When I Needed You The Most 4

A Millionaire Romance

Kia Jones

When I Needed You The Most 4

Copyright © 2022 by Kia Jones

All rights reserved.

Published in the United States of America.

Mailing List

To stay up to date on new releases, plus get information on contests, sneak peeks, and more,

Go To The Website Below...

www.colehartsignature.com

Flashback
Judy

This Is Who I Am

As I made some eggs for Marty, the phone was on a podcast station that monitored the stocks.

Over the summer, I'd become acquainted with financial literacy and other things to grow my individual wealth. A few of my investments had quick losses, but more had powerful gains. The pros definitely outweighed the cons. Though I focused a lot on my individual wealth, some of my investments were made from Poppa's account. This morning, I checked Poppa's account, and I'd grown it six percent. His moved faster because his accounts had more money to gamble with. Six percent wasn't much, but it was cool for two months.

After feeding Marty some eggs, I dropped him off at daycare and dropped Casey off with him. Since Lorena didn't live far, I helped her, and she helped me when needed. Like this morning, she had a viewing, so I took Casey when I took Marty.

Once back home, I cooked Poppa a big breakfast and made myself a smoothie instead. Since I heard him up and moving around upstairs, I went ahead and brought his food and coffee to him, just the way he liked.

Flashback

He was sitting on the edge of the bed, yawning, when I walked into our bedroom. I'd been giving him the cold shoulder since our son's birthday party five days ago. We both were busy this week, so I didn't have the time to confront him about what I had learned. To be real, going that route just wasn't making sense like it used to. What was the point? I didn't know what to believe at this point. All I knew was that I had started on a roll with who I was becoming and didn't want to let a bitch knock me off my game.

"Morning," I said as I placed the tray next to him.

He didn't respond, just stared at me like I had lost my mind as I made my way to the bathroom. I knew he expected me to hand him the tray and not just drop it next to him. This was what he would get from now on.

As I showered, I heard the fork tapping against the dinner plate, letting me know he was eating. As I got out, he was peeing, so he reached over, grabbed my robe, and tossed it to me so I didn't have to reach over him.

Without saying thank you, I grabbed the tray and carried it downstairs. While down there, I slipped on a tampon in the guest bathroom. Afterward, I cleaned. Once the dishes and kitchen were cleaned, I went back to our bedroom to get dressed.

Poppa stood in the bathroom door, just gazing down at me. Maneuvering around him, I tried to avoid eye contact, but he made it hard.

"I can feel you staring at me." I pushed past him and into the bathroom to do my makeup. He came and stood directly behind me, looking at me but not through the mirror. He didn't see me staring back.

"Where you going?"

"I have a meeting with a startup tech company that I'm investing in."

"You sure it's a good idea to do a startup?"

"It's my first one, so trust me, I've done the research." He didn't respond, just continued looking down at me like he was amused. His body was barely touching my back, but it still sent a chill down my spine. "Do you mind?" I dropped the lip liner and turned around.

"Do we need to talk?"

"No." I resumed applying my makeup.

"I'll beat'cho ass."

"Like to see you try."

"Man, give me some pussy before I go."

"I'm on my period," I said. That had been my excuse for the last five days. The first few days, I was lying, but I really started my period yesterday.

"Let me see." He had a smirk on his face, and I wanted to wipe it off.

"I'm bleeding, Poppa. Get away from me."

"Ight, remember that." He still didn't move.

"And what the fuck is so funny? You have that stupid smirk on your face like I'm a joke."

"When did you become a gangsta?"

"Go 'head. Leave me alone." I rolled my eyes. "You steady back there laughing, and I'm serious. That's your problem now. You don't take anything I say or do seriously."

"You talking like you really like that." He crossed both arms across his chest. The veins popped out in his strong, muscular arms. "You got some air in yo' chest?"

"Leave me alone. I refuse to be your entertainment this morning." He was still smiling. I couldn't stand him.

"Give me some pussy, then I'll leave you alone."

"No."

"You gon' make me take it?"

"If you want blood all over your dick, then go right ahead."

He didn't hesitate when he bent me over, knocking my makeup over. "Poppa, really?"

He glanced at me through the mirror. "Shut up."

"I'm serious, Marcel. I can't move." He had me pinned against the counter.

"What you moving for anyway?" He snatched my robe off. His hand found the string of the tampon and pulled it out. He held it up to verify the blood on it, then leaned over and tossed it into the toilet before flushing it.

"See? It's blood. Now move."

The corner of his lip curled upward as he gritted his teeth. "I don't give a fuck about no blood." He pulled his dick from his briefs and entered me without a second thought. Any other time, he gently eased inside, but now he was slamming into me. I would be lying if I said he didn't heavily turn me on. I hated how much I was enjoying being fucked.

"You make me sick. My gooohhhh." My gloss and concealer had rolled into the sink from the force of me moving back and forth.

"Yeah, I know." His hand reached around, grabbing my chin from behind, forcing me to give him eye contact in the mirror. "Why you being so mean to daddy?" I didn't respond, so he dug deeper inside me.

"Aaahhh, Poppa. Fuck."

"Huh? Why you being so mean to daddy?"

"I'm sorry."

"You don't love daddy?"

"I love you. My gooohhh. I love you."

He stuck two fingers in my mouth and pulled my head back against his body. "Tell daddy you love him."

"I love you, daddy."

"This pussy mine?"

"Yes."

He slammed into me, squeezing my breasts with his free hand. "Yes, what?"

"Yes, daddy, this pussy is yours."

"You gon' stop being mean to me? Huh?"

"Yes, daddy." He was fucking the common sense right out of me.

"Don't ever hold my pussy from me again. You hear me?" His hand was now wrapped around my neck.

"I hear you, daddy. Yes, I hear you, daddy."

"You want me to cum?"

I nodded. "Please."

He pulled my head back and stuck his mint-tasting tongue in my mouth. "I love you, girl." He picked up the pace, causing me to cum because I knew he was about to.

After we both came, he pulled his manhood out of me and said, "Hand me that towel right there."

Out of breath, still filled with ecstasy, I grabbed the wash towel and handed it to him. He wiped the blood from his dick and from my thighs.

He watched as I reached to grab a fresh tampon from the bottom cabinet. "Do you mind? I'm trying to put this on."

"I just stuck my whole dick in that lil' bloody pussy. Judy, if you don't put that shit on and shut up."

"Whatever." I slid it on as he watched.

He shook his head and headed for the door. "Gon' make me beat'cho ass," he said under his breath.

After taking another shower and getting dressed, I went to my meeting and still made it thirty minutes early. As I waited, I battled with mixed emotions. I wanted Poppa so bad, but I just wasn't sure if he was honest with me about his relationship with Gabriella. I could've asked five days ago about her, but I was afraid that maybe Agasha was right. Or maybe the two got closer after I beat her ass. That's what made more sense to me, and *that's why an affair with her would break my heart. Because if that was the case, I had literally pushed her right into my man's arms.*

After the meeting, I advised the chairman of the startup to reach out to my lawyer to see what else we could work out. I was given new information that changed the scope of our contracts.

Lorena told me to meet her for lunch after her last viewing in the afternoon, so we met downtown. Since Nadia called and said she was free, I invited her so we could discuss the next person we would help. It was a woman in Dallas who killed her rapist. She was black and a prostitute, on top of the fact that the man was a cop. She had no money for a lawyer, and this case was too big for a public defender. They would bury her.

Nadia chose not to drink, of course. She could barely keep water down. "Have you talked to the father?" Lorena asked, still not all the way hip to the details about Saw.

"Actually, no, I haven't."

"You keeping it?"

"Duh, Lorena."

Lorena frowned. "I'm sorry, Nadia. I just thought—"

"It's fine. Don't worry about it, but yes, I'm keeping it. I have my first doctor's appointment tomorrow."

"Then why don't you look excited?" I asked.

"You know why."

"I'm sure he will come around."

"He won't. I know he won't."

"I have to use the bathroom." Lorena grabbed her purse and quickly walked away with her knees clenched like she was about to go right then and there.

Nadia made sure she was gone and leaned in. "Can you ask Poppa to reach him?"

"I can. You know I will."

She then shook her head. "No, never mind. Don't do it. I'll just break my own heart."

"How?"

She tilted her head and frowned. "You know how." She took a small sip of water. "He's not going to be there."

"We don't know that for sure."

"I'm scared he's going to make me abort it. So, please don't tell Poppa. Promise me you won't tell Poppa."

"I promise."

"I'm so serious, Judy. Don't. I honestly believe he will make me kill it."

"You have my word."

Lorena came back to the table. "Whew, wine just runs right through me."

After a couple more hours of running through the plans for the Dallas case and figuring out the bond, lawyers, and everything else, we all went our separate ways. I had to pull up on Liyza, so I asked Lorena to grab Marty when she picked up Casey. Liyza and I needed to have a long talk because her poor decision making was affecting me now.

Instead of going inside when I pulled up on Liyza, I decided we could talk in the car since it was such a nice day out.

The cool A/C blew as I puffed on a blunt. My mood was ruined when Liyza slid into the passenger seat, arguing on the phone with Tay. I had noticed the only time she and Tay had problems was when Liyza ran out of money, which was why I was there. She was about to ask for another lump sum of money, acting like she missed me. She really thought I was stupid or something.

"Dumb bitch," she said as she hung up the phone. "I can't stand her, bro." She jerked her head toward me and clapped her hands together. "Do this look like a cold sore on my lip? Can't

even tell, right?" she asked, using her hand to point at the bump on her lip.

"Yeah, I can tell. Why?"

"Man, damn."

"What?" I wanted to pass her the blunt, but that blister on her lip looked nasty. To make matters worse, it seemed like she had been picking at it.

"Remember when I asked you to Uber me to the hospital the other day?"

I shook my head and sighed. "Please don't say what I think you're about to say."

"The bitch gave me syphilis. I took the meds, but the bump still showing."

"It don't happen that fast. It will go down, but damn." I passed her the blunt. "Gone kill that for me," I said, letting her know I didn't want it back.

She took a few puffs and calmed her nerves. Then she asked me what I knew she had dragged me out there for. "Listen, I need some money."

"For what? I thought you were working."

She blew me off. "Mane, I quit that damn job."

"Why?"

"I wanted to spend more time with Tay and the kids."

"What the fuck? Nah, that's not why." I shook my head, refusing to let her feed me bullshit. "You did it because you want to be up her ass twenty-four-seven."

"I know you not judging me," she said, raising her voice.

"Judging you? No! You're my friend, and I hate to see you going out sad and looking stupid. You have syphilis, for Christ's sake!"

"You want to yell at me for being stupid? You're literally with a man who uses you as a cum rag."

"Are you fucking serious? You want to go there with me?"

She had actually hurt my feelings. What she did next hurt my feelings even more.

"Just give me the money, Judy, damn!" She yanked my purse from me and started rambling through it.

It took me a few seconds to react because of the shock. Once the initial shock set in, I snatched my purse from her. "Are you crazy?!"

She started to hyperventilate and said, "Fuck this shit." Then she opened the car door.

"Where you going?" I jumped out of the car to follow her.

She turned to me and pushed me against my car. "It's not even your money. It's Poppa's fucking money. That little shit you be helping with don't even faze you, and you know it. Why won't you just help me?"

"That doesn't mean it's a free ride for those around me. I gave you over fifteen thousand dollars this summer."

"That's nothing to Poppa. It's his money," she said again, walking up on me.

"It doesn't matter, Liyza. Are you okay? Have you lost your damn mind?" Using all my strength, I pushed her away from me.

"You know she makes me happy."

"So, that means you're going to buy her?"

"I don't have a choice. What am I supposed to do? Let these niggas have her? I need her, Judy. You don't understand." She backed away and bit down on her fist with the other hand on her hip.

"Are you on drugs?" I snatched her arm and answered my own question. The track marks were right there.

"No." She snatched her arm back.

"I know what track marks look like, Liyza. You lying to me now? You fighting me now?" I stepped back with both hands behind my head. "You stealing from me now?"

"I didn't steal shit."

"You just grabbed my purse. If I hadn't stopped you, I know you would've run with it."

"Judy, just give me the money. I don't need the lecture. I'm getting a new job next week. All I need is to get back on my feet."

"Do the drugs help you cope with this? With Tay?"

"I don't know. Just give me the money." She moved quickly toward me like she had a great idea. "I'll pay you back. Yeah, I'll pay you back in installments."

As she rambled on and on, I got back into my car. She didn't even notice that I wasn't in front of her anymore until I walked back with some money in my hands. "Just take it. Get some help, Liyza. Please." I gave her all I had in cash, which was about three grand, and left.

The sun was going down by the time I made it to pick up Marty from Lorena's house. Liyza had stressed me so bad that I couldn't immediately get out of the car. For a few minutes, I just sat there. A part of me felt this was my fault. All the signs were there, but instead of helping her, I just flooded her with money. I should've gotten her help instead.

There was a knock at the window. It was Lorena. I unlocked the door and let her in. "What's wrong?" she asked.

I explained to her what had gone down with Liyza and me. This wasn't my first time venting about Liyza to her. "You ever thought that maybe you and Liyza have outgrown each other?"

"You sound like Poppa."

"I think you should definitely get her some help, but consider the fact that you and her have outgrown each other."

"She's been my friend since we were kids."

"History doesn't mean you have to deal with this."

"I know. I just don't know what to do."

She gave me the number of a few rehab facilities around town and brought my sleeping son to me.

Once back at home, I put him down for bed and went into me and Poppa's bedroom. Surprisingly, he was there, just brushing his teeth. "Poppa, are you fucking Gabriella?" I couldn't hold it in any longer.

He spit the toothpaste out. I thought he was about to flip, but he remained calm, which also surprised me. "Nah, but I know why you think that."

"Why?" I undressed and placed my clothes in the dirty laundry basket.

"She came to the party uninvited, for one. Two, your mother overheard the conversation you and Gabriella had over vodka and how upset you were. When I confronted her, she cried and said it was a joke." He wiped his mouth with a towel. "I fired her, and she slapped me."

I exhaled and turned the shower on. "And you choked her." I stepped inside.

"Yeah, how you know?"

"I saw her with a ring around her neck. I mean, like a handprint. She was crying."

"I gave her two weeks to find a new job."

"Why was she in Miami with you?"

"She wasn't. That's the part that pissed me off."

"I saw the pictures."

"If she was there, it wasn't for me. Never saw her in Miami."

"How did she know you were there?"

"She works for me, pretty girl. How else she gon' know?" He started to walk out but doubled back like he'd just thought of something. "Wait, that's why you been mean to me?"

"Can you stop saying it like that?"

"Like what?"

"I have not been mean."

"That's why? Come on, pretty girl, you know I got you. I thought we had trust?"

"We do. I just, I don't know. I'm sorry."

He looked down at the floor. "I'm getting real tired of you not trusting me."

"But she said—"

"Fuck what these bitches saying, Judy. I'm your man, and I've always been honest with you. Haven't I?" Frustration was written all over his face.

"Yes, it's just that, baby, you were gone with her for a while on that road trip that time. Then she was posting pics online."

"Maybe because she knows you've been on her page."

"How would she know?"

"Cherry Blossom?" he asked. "Really? Y'all couldn't pick a better name?"

"She told you?"

"Yeah, she told me."

"Why you didn't tell me she told you that?"

"That's girl drama, Judy. I don't fuck around with that. It wasn't that serious to mention it to you. Not until now. You really don't trust me, then what the fuck we even doing?" He waited for an answer. "Huh?"

"I'm sorry, baby. I know I have a bad habit of listening to other people, but we don't have the best track record. You cheated with Maddy."

"I know, and I've apologized for that so many times, pretty girl."

"I know you have." His puppy dog eyes made me feel sad. He really had turned his entire act around, and I still made it like it wasn't good enough.

"I want to move forward, but you ain't gon' let us."

"Everything was adding up, baby. You have to understand."

"You got a rich nigga from Haiti. That bitch wasn't the first

to tell you something, and she won't be the last. You gon' keep taking the words of other people over me? When have I ever lied to you? Ever?"

"Never."

"What? I can't hear you."

"I said never."

He backed toward the door. "That night at dinner, when I told you to find out if you loved me or not, you remember that?"

"Yes."

"Remember how I said I would know?"

"Yes." Lord, please. Please. Don't let him do what I think he's about to do.

"I know."

"You know what, Marcel?"

"You don't love me. If you did, you would trust me."

"Marcel..."

"We need some time apart. I ain't perfect, but damn, I'm tired, pretty girl."

"Tired?" I asked.

He took a deep breath. "I can't keep doing this with you."

"What do you mean? Baby, I trust you. I love you."

"You don't. I can't keep doing this with you. We need some time apart."

Chapter 1
Nadia
The Signal

"Wow. That's really a baby," I said as I watched the small, alien looking baby on the ultrasound screen.

"Yep. You're measuring about nine weeks, which lines up with your last period," the doctor said as she smiled. "Would you like pictures?"

"Yes, please." Before I knew it, tears were falling, and I wasn't planning to do that.

"Oh, here you are, darling," she said, handing me a tissue. She was an older black woman with a warm and welcoming smile. She looked like an aunt of mine back in Haiti who held all the family functions because she kept in touch with everyone.

"When's the due date?"

"March fourteenth, lovely. Would you like to set another appointment for next month? Everything looks fine and healthy, so no need for weekly appointments."

"Yes ma'am."

As she talked to me and explained everything I already knew, my brain fogged, causing me not to hear much of anything she was saying.

When I made it home, the kids were still at school, so I took the time to show my mother her new grandchild.

My mother was a stubborn woman and was still upset about our last talk, but she couldn't keep her excitement to herself. "I hope it's a girl."

"I have enough girls. I want a boy. You know? Balance it out."

"What will you name it if it's a boy?"

"I don't know yet. Great question." I sat next to her on the couch.

"Why do I have the feeling you'll be raising this baby without the father?"

"I have the same feeling."

She pushed herself from the couch. "Oh, you got a package earlier."

"Where?"

"I signed for it and put it on your bed. I have to sleep, but I want to talk about some things when I have the energy." She walked away and into her room.

When I made it to my room, the box was on my bed, unopened. I used my key chain to slice through the tape, only to find a single card.

It had a baby with congratulations typed in blue and pink. When I checked to see who it was from, my heart skipped a beat.

It was from: The Signal.

Chapter 2
Nadia
You Would Think I've Grown

Four months later...

Bringing the new year in with my family here in America was my dream, so why did I feel so numb? My fourteen-year-old daughter, Chance, watched TV as everyone else slept.

We all had remained awake until midnight to do the countdown and right after, they all went to sleep. My mother was the first to go.

Chance amazed me every day. She looked so much like her sister, Ayshan. Maybe because Ayshan was a replica of me.

"Okay, Mom. I'm off to bed." Chance stretched and came over to give me a cheek kiss.

"I think I'm taking it in too."

After turning the lights out, I grabbed some water and headed to bed. My life had grown boring, exactly what I feared. Judy said I should date to get Saw out of my system, but men didn't want to date pregnant women. They only wanted to fuck us.

As I cradled my growing belly, my cellphone rang once. A

few seconds later, it rang again. A few seconds later, it rang again but all the way through this time.

"Hello?" I said to the unknown caller.

"Hey, my beautiful baby mother." It was Saw. I knew that tone anywhere. His voice hadn't been heard to my ears since the last time I'd seen him face to face. The last signal I got from him was the note telling me congratulations.

"Saw."

"I know, I know. I'm sorry for not reaching out sooner. How have you been?"

"Well, it's a boy and I'm six, almost seven months pregnant."

"That's nice, but I asked how *you* were doing."

"Oh, so you care?"

He sighed. "Nadia, I can't talk to you as much as I want, and I spent a great amount of time drilling that into your head. Why can't you just go easy on me?"

"I'm sorry, but are you pregnant and going through it alone? Are you dealing with pregnancy hormones? Are you lonely? Are you about to have to raise another child who won't have both parents? No!"

"What you want me to say?"

"Why am I in this position again, Saw?"

"Because we both chose to make love to each other."

"Why would you get me pregnant knowing you couldn't be here?"

"Nadia?"

I had just remembered to breathe in and out. "I'm sorry. It's just so much going on in my head."

"What did you decide to name him?"

"Are you mad at me?"

"Why would I be mad?"

"Because I didn't get an abortion."

4

"I would never be mad about that. I'm so happy you decided to keep him. He was innocent in this."

"The only innocent one," I countered. "It's just so much. My nose is spreading. My ass is huge. Like why am I this big at six months? I was never this big at six months."

"Because you've been eating fried chicken every day."

"I don't even want to know how you know that." I laughed it off.

"I've told my wife about the baby."

My heart could've stopped. Hearing his voice when he said that put me on a different level because he didn't sound too happy about it. "What's her take on it?"

"She's upset, of course, but she's prepared to raise and be there for him like she was for Ayshan."

"Excuse me?"

"What?"

"My son won't be raised by you and her."

"I'm sorry—I just thought—I thought since..."

"What, Saw? What did you think?"

"The last time I saw you, it seemed like you were done raising children. Don't be upset, Nadia, please. I was just prepared to take him if you felt overwhelmed, that's all."

"I do feel heavy in the heart but I'm not giving my son up. I want you to understand that."

"That's completely fine. I understand and I'm sorry for upsetting you. I didn't know."

"How's Ayshan?"

"She's fine and she's also excited about her new sibling."

"She has several. Didn't think she'd be too over the top about mine."

"She's the most excited about yours because it's her first sibling that isn't a half sibling. Those were her words."

"Well, when it's looked at that way, I guess I understand."

"Have you told your mom?"

"She lives here, of course."

"Don't play stupid, you know what I mean."

"Yes, she knows you're the father, if that's what you want to know."

"Thanks for being honest."

"My mother didn't tell anyone." Though I sounded so sure, I wasn't. My mother had just started a job at a nursing home and there was no telling what she'd ran her mouth about.

"I believe you."

Not wanting to dwell on that subject, I moved the topic along to something else much more important. "I can't seem to get you off my mind. I know you can't call or be around as much as we would like, but Saw, I'm pregnant. At some point, you can't use your likings as an excuse."

"My likings?"

"The things you do around the globe."

"My likings," he said as if he had just now understood what I meant, and he wasn't pleased.

"Listen, I need to see you. I can't do this."

"I have to go."

"Saw, wait—"

The phone disconnected. Next time I was to hear his voice again would be when my son was born, and I knew that.

Chapter 3
Judy
On My Own for Real

As I sat at the dinner table with my mom and her family, one thing was for sure: I didn't belong here. My mother had finally decided to introduce me to her family and it was going just how I thought it would.

I had four siblings: Wanda, Camille, Jason, and Michael. Michael was the youngest and a teenager so he rarely ever left his room. Like now, he had grabbed his plate and ran up the stairs.

My mother had cooked Sunday dinner after the new year and I wished I would've stayed home. Wanda, who was twenty-five, married with a son, and a pediatrician, was my biggest problem at the moment. She sat right across from me, not hiding her disdain for me. Her dad, my mother's husband, was white so Wanda took a lot of his features. She had long, blonde hair, blue eyes, and a nice shape. A shape like an athlete would have. It was obvious she played some kind of sport in high school. She and I both had my mother's features but, of course, she was lighter than me. They all were lighter than me.

"So, why did you give Judy up for adoption?" Wanda asked, causing our sister Camille to gasp.

Camille was twenty-three with a black boyfriend who

played for the NFL. She was more down to earth than Wanda. "Why would you think now was the right time to ask that?" Camille asked her.

"I just want to know." Wanda shot her attention to our mother, who had a mug on her face I had never seen since the day we met. "I mean, is it because of her dad? Who was her dad? Does she know who her dad is? Or will we never know?"

"Wanda, that's enough," her husband said to her.

"Mom?" Wanda continued. "Are you sure she's yours?"

"What's that supposed to mean?" I broke my silence.

"I mean, it's no secret you're darker than the rest of us. Why come around now?"

"Wanda!" Camille was now on her feet.

"They're right, Wanda. You need to relax," Donnie, my mother's husband, had said. His face was red and flushed with embarrassment.

"What made you want to come around now? For money?"

There was a loud bang against the table. Our mother had finally had enough. "Wanda, excuse yourself," she said in a sweet tone. I'd spent months alone with my mother so I knew there was a side to her that she left behind, but Wanda was about to see.

"Excuse myself?" Wanda asked, looking at her dad for confirmation.

Donnie nodded and dropped his fork. "I think you need to take a walk."

"Wow." She forced a laugh and tossed her napkin into her unfinished food. "A bastard comes around and everyone loses their mind."

"Get the fuck out of my house," my mother finally yelled. Wanda hesitated at first but did as she was told after a few seconds of hard staring.

"Let's go," she said to her husband, who was already

halfway out the door. Even he was embarrassed by her behavior.

"We don't have any money for you," Wanda said, throwing one last bell before heading out.

"We're sorry about her. She's just used to being the oldest and she just found out about you, so it's a lot to take in," Donnie said, attempting to smooth it over.

"That's no excuse for her behavior, Dad," Camille said.

"Maybe I should just go." As I stood and backed away from the table, everyone begged me to stay.

"What? No, you can't leave," my mother said, now on her feet and walking around to me, but I was already near the door.

"Judy, please don't go." Camille had now begun to follow behind me. They both were on my heels until the minute I got to my car.

Both Camille and my mother were deeply apologetic and hated to see me go, but I didn't stay. As I drove away, they both held each other and watched until I disappeared down the street. I couldn't wait to get to Poppa's loft and relax. I don't know what I was even thinking trying that out. From what my mother had told me about her new family, I should've known it would go something like it just did.

Soon as I made it downtown, my mother called but I ignored her. Then Camille called. Then my youngest brother. Finally, Donnie called. He must have been a last resort since I wasn't answering. It was a rainy day out but the rain had stopped just enough for me to run inside without getting wet. The front desk agent knew me so she went ahead and beeped me up on the elevator.

Once in front of his door, I took a deep breath. It had been so hard to see him away from our home, but this was our life now. For the last four months it had been our life. It still amazed me that once he left that day, he really never came back. I never expected that.

"Come in," he said as he stepped to the side.

Just as I fixed my mouth to ask where Marty was, he came stumbling from around the corner with his arms out and smile beaming. "Mama!"

I put my purse on the kitchen cabinet and squatted down. "Hey, baby." No matter how bad I was feeling, my son always made me feel so much better. It's like every day was something new with him. He was starting to grow so fast.

"Look." He handed me a hundred-dollar bill, and I giggled.

"Where'd you get this?"

"Must've been in my closet again, going through my shoes." Poppa took the money from him.

"You have money in your shoes?"

"Na, it falls out of the pants into my shoes sometimes, I guess. How was your mother's?"

"Left early and didn't eat. Wanda made shit weird."

Marty climbed down and ran over to the couch to watch TV as Poppa pulled a pan of food from the oven.

"That's why I made these oxtails and cabbage for you."

I smiled because I loved oxtails and he knew that. We both did. "Why?"

"You was never gon' stay the whole dinner."

Smiling and leaning back, I said, "Please tell me you have wine."

"I got you." He looked so sexy in his maroon-colored jogger suit. Today, like most days, he kept it simple and wore a small chain around his neck with a watch. As he sat the wine bottle and glass in front of me, he caught me staring and smirked. "Gone on."

"What? I can't look at you."

"What you looking at me for?"

"You sexy, that's all."

"You want another baby or something?"

"Hush."

"A'ight then. Keep giving me compliments, gon' have your ass right in labor and delivery in nine months." He slid a glass plate in front of me and put a healthy amount of food onto the plate. He even added rice.

"This is amazing." I took a bite before he was even done placing all the food onto the plate.

"I'm already knowing. So what happened?" He leaned back and crossed his arms around his chest, giving me his undivided attention.

"Wanda hates me."

"She seems like the type."

"It's like she takes it to the head that she looks white. She tried to pull a race card and mention my skin color, it was weird." I thought back on Camille, who didn't look as white as Wanda did. She must have felt deeply offended also. Wanda was the type to not care who was hit in her crossfire, as long as she burned her target.

"How's your mother?"

"She's fine. Oh, and she asked about you. She said just because you and I are taking a break doesn't mean you can't check in on her. She said she misses you two's morning chats."

"Tell her I said bet. I got her."

"Poppa, when you coming home?" I asked this every other week, but lately I'd asked every time we talked.

"Don't start."

"No, for real. We still love each other?"

"Correct." The grin on his face made me want to punch him. He grinned even harder when he noticed I wasn't smiling. "What, baby? I'm tired of having this conversation over and over. Aren't you?"

"Whatever."

"I'm coming home, pretty girl. I just don't feel like it's the right time."

"Okay, but you left because I couldn't trust you and don't you think it's making it even harder to trust you now? Now that you're away? Baby, come on."

"I know. So what's up? You been okay?"

I sighed. He always avoided these hard conversations. "Never mind."

"Don't be like that. You know I ain't going nowhere."

"I know, but it's like, am I that bad that you don't want to come home? Really?"

"I signed a six-month lease."

"You don't give damn about this lease and you know it."

"I'm saying, it can be a time marker for us. At the end of my lease, I'll be home and hopefully we don't have to go through anything like this again."

"You're such an asshole. You dating someone?"

"You know I ain't."

"I don't know anything, Poppa."

"I'm *telling* you I'm not seeing anyone so you should believe me. I don't lie to you and I never have." He was growing impatient so I decided to change the subject.

"Nadia's due date is coming up."

"I know."

"Does *he* know?" I asked, speaking of Saw.

"Of course."

"Should've known. He knows everything."

"Judy?"

"Yes?" I made eye contact with him again.

"You know I love you, right?"

"I know."

"Just keep knowing that. Nothing and nobody comes

before you. I'm not seeing anyone. I'm not fucking anyone. I work. Gabriella is fired and has been for a while. Thankfully, you stepped up and took her place and you've been doing an amazing job." It was true. After firing Gabriella, he didn't have time to find someone else so I filled the slot. It was only supposed to be temporary but he and I actually liked it. I didn't have to be in the office. I could work from home since all calls and emails came to his work phone, which I now had control of, too.

"Thank you for the reassurance."

"I understand you need more of that and I'm willing to do it. But from the comfort of my own home for now. Okay?" He leaned down and passionately kissed me.

"Okay."

"I love you and I have to go to a property. They're having a pipeline problem." He grabbed his keys from the drawer. "Lock up after you leave."

"Okay."

After he left, I gathered Marty's belongings and headed out the door.

I liked where Poppa and I were right now but I loved when he was with me every day. This time alone had taught me to love me and my son a little more and it also taught me to trust him. I had no choice but to trust him and take his word. He even gave me a key to prove that he was all about me. I couldn't let Maddy haunt me like this.

Marty was sleep by the time I got home so I walked slowly to not wake him up. The rain started to fall but I had an umbrella. Times like this I needed my man here. He would've grabbed Marty for me and made sure I didn't touch an umbrella or a door.

I had too much stuff in my hand, so I couldn't lock the door immediately. After quickly laying Marty down on the couch and turning toward the door, I got the shock of my life. It's like I had just seen a ghost.

She stood in the entryway of the door with water dripping from her body like she'd been out in the cold and rain for hours. She was shivering and shaking. Her weight loss scared me—she resembled a skeleton.

"Maddy?"

"I had nowhere else to go." She shivered so hard that it seemed like she was convulsing. So many thoughts ran through my mind, paralyzing me. Maddy had always haunted me so was that what she was doing now? Was she real? "I know you thought I was dead."

"You're really here." I stood still, contemplating if I wanted to attack or call the cops.

"I'm not here to hurt you, Judy. I had nowhere else to go and I don't know how to find Poppa."

"How did you find me?"

"I googled Marty's school and watched you pick him up the other day. Followed you here and ditched the car I had been in. Someone's trying to kill me and I need your help."

"I can't help you."

Her eyes were no longer full of hatred. Now they were sunken and low, full of sadness. "Please, Judy. Someone wants me dead and I can't figure out who. Not many people knew I was still alive."

"So if they want you dead, won't they try and kill me?"

"That's the thing. I don't know who it is. They tried to kill me in Haiti."

The cold breeze made me realize the front door was still open so I rushed over to shut it. "Jesus, I can feel the cold on you when I walk by," I said as I hurriedly tossed blanket from the couch onto her.

"I tossed out some soup that I no longer wanted by giving it to my cat. I always give her soup. Within two minutes of her eating it, she died." She went on and on as I led her to the sofa.

"What if she was allergic?"

"Everything in my fridge was poisoned. I know it. The next day, I left home to go and get more food and it went up in flames the second I stepped out." She showed me a scar on her back. "I made it out just in time."

"Maybe it was bad timing."

She grabbed my hand tightly and harshly stared into my eyes. "Someone is trying to kill me, Judy."

"Okay, let me just call Poppa and we can sort this all—"

"No! Don't call him yet! Please. I need to rest and think clearly before reaching out to him."

"You want to stay here?"

"Someone wants me dead and you're the only one I can trust."

I wanted to let her back out onto the cold streets of Austin but I just couldn't do it. My heart wouldn't let me.

"I'll get the guest bedroom ready for you. First, let me make you some soup."

Chapter 4
Nadia
Another Little Me

It had been four days since I'd heard from Saw and for four days, he was all I could think about. Hearing his voice made me happy but seeing him would do more.

As always, everyone in the house was sleep with the exception of Chance. She was cuddled up under me, rubbing my stomach as we watched TV. Lately, I'd seen a different side of her. Back when her father was alive, all I got was an angry teenager who hated the world and everyone in it. Now she was so nurturing and at my beck and call.

Knock. Knock. Knock.

My heart fluttered when I realized someone was indeed at my window. To my surprise, Chance was the first out of bed but she wasn't in a panic like I was. In fact, she seemed to have known who it was. "Relax, it's Ayshan," she said calmly.

"Excuse me?" A lump was caught in my throat. Did she just say what I thought she did?

She smiled and lifted the window and sure enough, Ayshan came crawling through. She and Chance welcomed each other with a warm embrace. "Hi, Mom." Ayshan then met me with a big hug. "Hi, little brother." She cradled my stomach.

"What the fuck?"

Chance put her index finger over her mouth. "Shhh." She gently closed and locked my bedroom door.

"You got the stuff?" Ayshan asked her.

Chance surprised me when she went under my bed and pulled out a small device. "It's the only one I could find."

"What's this?" I wanted to know. "Is that a bomb?"

"No, of course not. It's something to help with signal," Chance said.

"Okay, so what's going on?"

"Oh," Ayshan said like she'd just remembered I had no idea what I was going on. "A couple of months back, I watched Chance at school. Thought I was being discreet but she walked right up to the car I had borrowed and knew I was watching her."

"How did she know?"

"She looks identical to you," Chance said. "I knew it couldn't have been a coincidence."

"She also overheard you and your mother arguing about me one night so she knew she had a sister."

"Oh, wow," I said, embarrassed. "Do your sister and brother know?"

Chance shook her head. "Na, they have no idea." The way Chance maneuvered so comfortably around Ayshan, I knew they had been in frequent contact.

"How do you two talk? Over the phone?"

Chance lightly chuckled. "Oh no. We have a couple times but that's not how we mainly communicate. We use different things."

"Like?"

"Morse code when she uses free radio stations."

"How do you know which radio station?"

"Mom, come on. Let's talk about something else," Ayshan said, taking things from her bag. The first items were digital procure frames. "I got these for you. They have cameras on them. Dad wants one in your room and one in the living room."

"Absolutely fucking not."

"Mom, please. You can have your privacy it's just that something has come up and he wants to make sure everyone here is safe."

"What's come up?"

"Mom?" Chance said.

"What?"

"Just please don't be difficult. You're pregnant and really annoying these days. Please don't choose now to be annoying. I don't know much about Saw but from what I've heard, he wouldn't ask for these to be put up unless it was absolutely necessary."

Sighing, I rubbed my belly and gave in. "Okay."

After we placed the picture frame in the living room, Ayshan requested to see her grandmother and siblings as they slept. "Should we wake them? You know, so they can meet you," I whispered as we stood by the door to the kids room.

"No, Mom. I've already said this over and over."

"But you met with Chance."

"Chance is older and just no." She walked back to my bedroom and waited for me and Chance.

"I'm sorry. I just thought since you revealed yourself to Chance..."

"You thought you would get an inch and take it a mile. Mom, I'm not here for a family gathering. I'm here because someone is back from Haiti and I'm afraid she might come for you."

"Who?"

"Maddy."

I swallowed the bile that had piled up. "Maddy?"

She studied my face. "You knew she was alive. Didn't you?"

"Yes, but in Haiti."

"Dad attempted to delete her twice but she escaped both attempts."

"How do you know?"

"I last tracked her entering Texas."

"Your dad sent you?"

"No, he didn't. He tried to stop me but as you know, I can't be stopped." She and Chance laid in bed with me—Chance on one side and Ayshan on the other. Both rubbing my belly. It almost felt like a dream. "I need to find her."

"I'm the very last person that would know."

"I think she may be with Judy."

"Nonsense. Judy believes Maddy is dead and even if she didn't believe that, there's no way Judy would help her."

"You sound so sure."

"I am."

"I know she's not with Poppa."

"How are you so sure?" I asked her.

"Poppa would've killed her."

"Maybe she's already dead then."

"She's not but she needs to be. She's causing a lot of uproar back in Haiti with her rumors and conspiracy theories."

"She's been talking. Of course." Maddy was like a parasite. She sunk into things. She poisoned those who held her close and attempted to help her. She drained people of life.

"We need her gone. She poses a bigger threat than anyone could ever imagine."

"Oh, trust me, I know." I thought back on how she lured me into something that was supposed to be my fate. I knew how dangerous she was.

"Have you killed before?" Chance asked.

"I don't think that's an appropriate question for Ayshan," I said.

"I wasn't asking Ayshan."

I underestimated Chance. She, too, was another little me.

Chapter 5
Judy
The Girl in the Horror Movies

The look on Maddy's face when she realized she was no longer in a bedroom was priceless. When she first realized the chains, she almost puked. "Where am I?"

"Relax. You're in the basement."

"The what? How the fuck did you get me in a basement?"

I nodded over to a sleeping bag. "Dragged you. I'm actually very pleased that you didn't wake up. You lie about everything but you didn't lie about being exhausted."

She looked as if she wanted to reason with me and then strangle me. "Judy? This isn't you. You have to let me go."

"I don't have to do shit."

She took a few deep breaths and then screamed. "Help!"

I couldn't help but chuckle. "Are you serious? Nobody can hear you and even if someone could hear you, anybody that I know wants you dead." I shook my head. "Idiot."

"You bitch!"

I tossed some toast and a boiled egg on the mattress. "Doesn't feel good to be locked in a basement, huh?"

She kicked the food on the floor. "Fuck you."

"I wouldn't have done that if I were you. I need to take my son to school and run some errands. Won't be home till later, so if you can reach the food, have at it." I walked halfway up the stairs and turned around. "This might be the biggest test of all from me and honestly, I don't know if I'm going to pass."

"No! No! Don't leave me down here! No! Please!"

I closed the door on her and got Marty ready for school. I didn't know what I was going to do with her yet. Last night I contemplated killing her in her sleep but I didn't have the heart to. The only thing I could think to do was to tell Poppa about it.

Shortly after dropping Marty off at school, I went to Poppa's place. He was in the shower when I let myself in.

As I sat on the toilet and watched the water drip from his sexy body, intrusive thoughts plagued my mind. Like what if I starved her to death or drowned her in our pool.

"Fuck you grinning at?" Poppa asked, snatching me back to reality. The guilt immediately sat inside. This wasn't me. I wasn't a killer. All I had to do was the right thing, but what was the right thing? Letting her go could put us in danger again. The last person that tried to help her almost got murdered. But I couldn't tell Poppa. He would surely kill her.

"Nothing," I said. "Just thinking."

"You never come over this early. Everything okay, pretty girl?" He pulled the towel from the rack and kept his eyes on me.

"Yes, just wanted to see you."

He smirked. "You must want some dick."

"I just miss you." When I realized that I couldn't tell him about Maddy, I decided against saying anything at all about her. I shouldn't have ever let her stay. Maddy was always a parasite in my life ever since the day I met her. Here she was reaching from the dead, confining me to yet another mental prison. Not this time. "I have to go." I hurried and walked away.

With water still dripping from him, he ran after me and

grabbed me from behind, kissing the back of my neck. "You're getting me wet," I complained.

"That's the plan."

"No, you're literally making me wet. Your entire body is soaking."

He grabbed me tighter. "What's wrong?"

"You're wet."

"Other than that."

"Nothing. I just have a lot on my mind."

He sat on the couch and pulled me into his lap. "Tell daddy what's wrong?"

It was right on the tip of my tongue. All I had to do was say it. That's all. I couldn't do it. "Nothing. I just wanted to see you before I started my day, that's all."

"You sure? I got a lil' minute before I have to leave out, so I can make your pussy tingle if you want."

"You play so much."

"Who said I'm playing?"

"I have to go."

"You came up here looking all good and kid free, now you want to leave?" I felt his dick bulging on my thigh. Any other time I would've been jumping all over it, but I had a woman chained in my basement.

"I have to go, baby." I stood and fixed my clothing. Still, I could feel him watching me from the couch. "What?"

"I know when something's wrong so just tell me."

"Nothing is wrong, baby."

He then relaxed onto the couch, stroking his hard dick. "You gon' leave your boy like this?"

"He will be okay. Gotta go." I quickly left out before he tried to stop me. For the first time ever, I wasn't in the mood to please him and it actually felt good. A smile crept on my face as the elevator took me down.

As I drove away, he called and I ignored it. Even that felt empowering.

Though I took my time getting home, I rushed into the house. I couldn't believe it. The woman who'd succeeded in making my life a living hell was at my mercy. If she lived or died was up to me, and the weight of it all felt like a painful euphoric experience.

She began screaming as soon as I turned the light on. "You bitch!" She'd puked everywhere and instead of using the bucket, she decided to shit in the bed. "Now you have to clean this up."

"I'm not and if you don't, I guess you'll sleep here."

The realization sat in that I was not the same Judy she'd left last year. Her face had seemingly deflated, looking more sunken than it did the day before. "I need food, Judy. And water."

Nodding at the boiled egg and toast that was still on the floor, I said, "You eat that before I give you anything else."

"You're kidding," she said, but it seemed more like a question.

"What happened the night you were supposed to be killed?"

"You would've loved that, wouldn't you?"

"What happened?"

"He took me away and told me if he was to ever see me again, I would die."

"He didn't kill you." I kept drilling that into my head now and all night before. I couldn't wrap my head around why I felt relieved but disappointed.

"He didn't kill me. Get over it. He loves me."

"If he loves you so much then why are you here?"

"You're so weak."

I pulled a foldable chair out and sat in it. "Yea? Explain."

"If I were you and you were me, I would've killed you the minute you walked through my door."

"Luckily, I'm nothing like you."

"And that's what makes you weak."

"Because I'm not a killer?"

"Because you're the girl that dies first in a horror movie."

Seeing her talk so much mess about me while sitting in her own shit amused me to say the least. "What girl are you in the horror movie?"

"I'm the monster."

"Monsters always die in the end," I said. She swallowed the lump in her throat and wiped the smirk off her face. "No slick come back?"

"How's he been?"

"Who? My man? *My man?*"

"How is Marcel?" She frowned and humbled herself. She missed him. Pathetic.

"He's fine. Just closed another deal. He's becoming quite the businessman. You know?" It was true and I was proud of him. Maybe I was so proud because I worked for him now and saw up close and personal how hard he worked and how much he worked.

"I love that for him. Has he asked about me?"

"No. Buuuut he *did* mention how you fucked something up in Miami last year. He had to go and fix it." She shook her head. "You remember?"

"Yea, I do. It was my mess to fix but he sent me off so fast."

"Awww," I said sarcastically. I couldn't recognize who I was right now.

"You feel so powerful sitting in that plastic chair looking down on me. Don't you?" She straightened her shoulders.

"I do."

"I should've killed you," she said.

Ding ding.

My doorbell rang. Before she could scream, I stuffed a sock in her mouth and put tape over it.

I was expecting to see Lorena maybe but not Nadia and Chance. I was so used to seeing Nadia wild and free. Seeing her pregnant with her teenage daughter on the side of her was new to me. She never came unannounced either, so that was also odd.

"Come in," I said, opening the door for them.

"Aunt Judy, I have to pee."

"Go ahead, baby. You know you don't have to ask."

She walked down the hall as Nadia and I sat on the couch. "I see you're getting bigger and bigger. You didn't look like this last week," I halfway joked.

"Did I tell you it was a boy?"

"Yes, you don't remember?" I sighed and looked around. "Nadia, is everything okay?" Could she be here because of Maddy? Na, she couldn't have been. How would she know Maddy was here?

"I just wanted to get out the house. With me being pregnant and dealing with my mom, I just had to get away. The kids are driving me crazy, too." She nervously laughed.

"I would think everything drives a pregnant woman crazy, or was that just me?"

"No, it wasn't just you." She laughed but it didn't seem genuine. Maddy had me paranoid. It was amazing how she rubbed off on me. "Do you have popcorn?" she asked.

"Popcorn?"

"Pregnancy craving."

I'd just noticed that I hadn't heard a toilet flush and Chance was nowhere to be found. "I got you." Since the basement door was on the way to the kitchen, I stopped by there and just in time. Chance had just lifted her hand to open the basement door. "What the fuck are you doing?" I asked before I knew it.

She flinched and turned to face me. I could always tell when children were up to something, but Chance looked really confused right now. "This isn't the bathroom?"

"You've been here plenty of times. When has the bathroom ever been in the basement?"

She snapped her fingers. "That's right. It's down the hall but the other way." She smiled and walked away. "It's been a minute."

"Yea, okay."

As I was in the kitchen, the doorbell rang again.

What the hell is going on?

I had never been this popular before. Why now? Were the people trying to kill Maddy now trying to kill me? Who were the people trying to kill her?

It was Poppa at the door. "Where is your key?"

"We will get going," Nadia said as she and Chance walked by.

"Wait, you just got here."

"It's fine, we have to get back to the house. My mom is calling me to come tend to my kids."

"Okay, well I owe you popcorn."

She nodded and they left. Poppa waited as I closed the door. "What's wrong?" He looked so sad standing in the foyer.

"I don't like the way you left earlier. Tell me what's wrong, pretty girl. Please." He grabbed my hand.

Huh?

I had to think of something. Poppa wasn't a stupid man so I couldn't just tell him anything and he'd believe it. The look on his face told me I needed to think fast before I found myself in a crazy position.

"I just miss you so much and us being apart is taking its toll.

There's no reason for us to live apart and I just been so depressed." I had been down, but not as down as I had just made it seem.

He pulled me in, rubbing the back of my head as I rested on his chest. "Why didn't you say that?"

"I've been telling you that for the longest."

"I'll come home. Okay? You're right, it's no reason for us to be apart. It's just that I've never seen that look on your face like I did earlier and it scared me."

"I'm sorry." I felt crazy crazy, crazier than I ever had. I didn't expect him to agree to come home. It had been four months and I still couldn't get him home but the day I don't need him here, he decided to come home.

I was fucked.

Chapter 6
Judy
Red Snakes

After Poppa left to drop Marty off the next morning, I went to the basement and fed Maddy. Just like I knew, she ate everything with much gratitude this time and she was less mouthy. I'd also left a rag, new bucket of warm water and bleach so she could clean around herself. The smell was beginning to make me and her sick.

After taking care of that, I set up Poppa's work schedule for the day and handled closing his lease at the loft. By the time all of that was done, it was time for me to feed Maddy lunch.

Today was actually a busy day because I also had to make time to pull up on Liyza. But before pulling up on her, I picked up Lorena. Ever since Liyza pulled that weird mess last time, I hadn't allowed myself to be alone with her anymore. I didn't trust the woman she was turning into. She's become bitter and resentful to any and everyone.

The minute we walked into her apartment, I could tell she hadn't left in days, maybe even weeks. It was dark and stuffy so I opened the back door to let some air inside.

"She took my kids from me, man," Liyza said as she puffed on a cigarette and laid back. Her hair was all over her head and there were a few bald spots.

"What kids?" Lorena asked.

"My boys."

"Those aren't your fucking kids. Are you going to keep finding reasons to be sad over this no good bitch? Are you crazy?" I asked, picking random shit off the floor. "And who dirty drawls is these?"

She leaned up and snatched them. "They mine."

"Have you been showering?" Lorena asked. Over the last four months, Liyza had grown accustomed to Lorena just as much as she was with me.

"I shower when I feel the need. I don't stink."

"Are you serious?" I wanted to know. She couldn't have been.

"I wash my ass when I'm on my period these days and that's it." Liyza put her head down again. "She took my boys from me, man."

Lorena shook her head and looked over at me. "Liyza, get the fuck up." Lorena waited for Liyza to stand but she didn't move so Lorena physically made her stand. "That bitch don't care about you! She gave you two STDs within two weeks! Wake up! Wake the fuck up." She let her go and Liyza instantly dropped back onto the couch.

I walked to the kitchen and busied myself with dishes to keep from seeing her like this. "You called me over to listen to you mope and groan about this lady?" She now had scratch marks all over her skin from it peeling. I had to get her into a rehab. Today was the cherry on top. It couldn't wait anymore.

"Actually, I needed a few dollars."

Lorena sighed and sat on the couch. "What's a few dollars?" I asked.

"Five thousand," she said so freely. Like it was five dollars she was asking for.

"What's half that?" Lorena asked me.

"$2500."

"Okay give her half of the half."

"What?" Liyza's voice peaked as she used an ashtray to put the cigarette out.

Lorena had been drilling into my head that I needed to set boundaries with Liyza. We had no boundaries and that's why Liyza felt so comfortable doing the things she did to me and saying the hurtful things she would say.

"I'm not giving you five thousand."

She stood and began complaining about all she was going through and how she was behind on bills. Same thing every week. "You know you can afford it. You know Poppa can afford it."

"See, and I hate when you do that. You're always getting upset with her about *her money*. And when she says no, you want to call it Poppa's money. It don't matter who's money it is, Liyza, it's not yours," Lorena said. I loved having Lorena with me because she didn't mind saying those hard things that needed to be said and doing what needed to be done. I would hesitate and Lorena would let the words flow like water with action to follow.

"Bitch, you shut the fuck up. I still ain't forgot how you accused me of stealing from you the other month."

"You did. I ain't crazy. Never in my life has anything ever came up missing until the Dayi left you alone in the car with my purse for a few seconds."

Liyza glanced at me and pointed at Lorena. "This bitch always got some shit to say about stuff that ain't got nothing to do with her. You peep this?"

"What she saying ain't wrong."

"She ain't right either! She talks to me like I'm trash and you just let her. You don't even know this bitch like that."

"I've been knowing Lorena a while now."

"Remember what happened with the last bitch you called a friend."

"Yea, look what happened to her," I said, throwing major shade at how she fucked me over and ended up dead. Wow, I was loving this new me. It didn't even make me feel bad when I said it.

"Oh, you threatening me, bitch?"

"Have you fucked me over?"

"What?"

"Listen, the point is, you're not getting five grand," Lorena interrupted us.

As they bickered back and forth, I contemplated on what I'd just told Liyza and came to the conclusion that I didn't feel bad about handling her this way. I could no longer be around her alone. That's where she and I were right now and she made it that way. Poppa told me that someone who had the nuts to steal from a friend was someone that could kill a friend. They had no respect. She had no respect for me. Somewhere along the line she lost it, but I was going to help her find it.

"Fine," I said, stopping the two of them from bickering.

Lorena turned to me disapproving as Liyza had a *boo-ya* look on her face to Lorena. "Fine what?" Liyza asked.

"I won't give you half of five grand."

She put her hand in Lorena's face. "See! You should have shut up and minded your business," she said as Lorena slapped her hand away.

"In fact, I won't even give you five grand."

They both turned back to me, realizing what was going on. "Huh?"

"As a matter of fact, I ain't giving you a dime."

"Stop playing so much."

"That's the problem, you're always under the impression

that anything about me is a joke. You're not getting any money from me but I *will* take you to rehab and foot the entire bill."

She stood and balled her fist like a tantrum throwing child. She even huffed and puffed like a little pig that wanted to blow someone's house down. "I told you it's for bills."

"The program I want to take you to is six months. It's very luxurious. You'll have your own room and it's way bigger than this apartment. You can have visits and the food is amazing."

"You can't just give me the money?"

She wasn't listening anymore. Any other time I would give in and just hand the money over, but not today. She was about to learn a valuable lesson about the woman I was becoming.

"Let's go, Lorena."

As I dried my hands, Lorena gathered her purse and something happened that had never happened. Liyza reached her hand back, slowly, and contemplated before slapping Lorena with the back of her hand. It caught all of us off guard. Even Liyza stepped back and looked at her hand like she didn't know where it came from.

Lorena grabbed her face and looked at Liyza as if she was gathering that this had really just happened. I tried so hard not to laugh. "Oh hell no." Lorena grabbed Liyza's shoulder to hold her in place as she slapped her over and over. She slapped her from the living room all the way to the kitchen where I was.

After laughing internally, I finally broke it up. Liyza kept trying to get around me until I grabbed her. "Stop! Fucking stop!"

"She just beat my ass in my own house!" She pointed at Lorena, who was equally as upset.

"Liyza, what the hell has gotten into you? Huh?"

Before she could answer, the front door swung open and in walked Tay. I could smell the weed and liquor before she made it past the threshold. "And where the hell have you been for three days?" Liyza asked, quickly forgetting what had just transpired.

Tay ignored her and walked to the fridge and grabbed some juice. She then turned to me like she'd been needing to tell me something. "I saw your fine ass baby daddy the other day."

"Where?"

"At a construction site. Looked like he as working."

"And what were you doing at a construction site?"

"My brother is a construction worker. I was picking up some money from him since I can't get mine from you these days." Tay shook her head like she was utterly disgusted with Liyza. Instead of a response, Liyza put her head down. "You want to be a man so bad but can't do what a man do. You can't fuck me. Least you can do is help me with groceries."

"Groceries, huh?" I asked.

She crossed her arms and rolled her neck. "Yes. Why?"

"How much are these groceries you need?" Lorena asked.

"Five thousand."

Me and Lorena sighed at the same time. Liyza exhaled in frustration like she didn't want me to know what the five grand was for. I already knew what it was for before Tay even said anything. It was common sense.

"You're never home so who needs it?" I asked.

"My boys. They're teenagers now and eat a lot."

"That's ridiculous. You need to get better at lying," Lorena said. It pissed people off that Lorena didn't sit around and let people bully her.

"Aren't you the one who has a baby by the mayor?" Tay asked.

"Tay?! Shut up, mane. You trippin'." Liyza said.

"Why would you think that?" Lorena asked, nearing her. I had ever told anyone that. So how did she know?

"Liyza saw a picture of the mayor holding your son. Either

you're a great outstanding citizen or he was at the birth because he's the father."

"You saw that picture? It's only a picture like that in my phone and in my wallet." She turned to mug Liyza. "I wonder who was in my wallet."

"It would be terrible if the press found out about that. I mean, you guys are doing so many great things in Texas for women. I would hate for a rumor like that to ruin it."

Before me or anyone else could say anything, Tay was gone with the wind and out the door. Liyza tried to run after her but Tay got out of there.

I couldn't even look at Liyza right now. Lorena and I left without saying a word. My days never turned out good whenever I went to see Liyza.

"I can't stand that bitch," Lorena said as we stopped at a stop sign.

"Me neither. Let's go to that burger place you took me to the other week with the good drinks."

"You remember how to get there? Take this back road." She pointed to the right of me. One thing about Austin, it wasn't short on wooded areas. It was so beautiful.

"I can't believe her."

"I can," she responded. "It's always the ones you help the most when they need it. Them the ones who get an inch and take it a mile every single time.

"I'm starting to feel like maybe she and I have outgrown each other. Though I still want to get her help, I just don't see this ending well with Tay."

As we drove down the scenic route, we noticed a car speeding up behind us. "What the fuck?" Lorena asked, turning around.

"Move fast," she said.

Luckily, I sped up. If I hadn't, the car would've rammed

into my bumper. The car finally sped on side of me, flagging me down. "This bitch," I said when I noticed it was Tay.

"She got some nerve. Pull over in front of that tree up there. Go past the ditch."

When I pulled over, Tay quickly got out the car and so did we. Before she even made it to us, we were meeting her at the rear of my car. "You must be crazy?" Lorena asked her with folded arms.

"I don't know how things like this go so I'll just say it—pay me or I go to the press."

Lorena laughed historically. "About what?"

"Let's start with the mayor's nigger love child and Judy's drug dealer boyfriend who started his empire at the expense of junkies. The same people y'all help. I'm sure the press would love that."

Lorena shook her head and walked away as I followed Tay back to her raggedy car. "Wait, come back." I caught her just before she got back into the car.

"I said what I said. I want three million in three days."

"Three days?!" I said. "That's not enough time."

"You're rich, work it out."

"Poppa is rich, not me. I can't just go asking him for three million dollars without a reason."

"Okay, so tell him."

"You don't want me to tell him. Trust me."

"What? He's going to kill me? Don't make me laugh."

It all happened so fast. I didn't even hear Lorena or see her walk by.

Tay's head swung against her car before she completely dropped to the ground. Blood quickly formed a pool around her. I hurried and jumped back, grabbing a shocked Lorena so blood wouldn't get on her shoes.

Lorena dropped the jack hammer. "What have I done?"

"No, pick that back up," I said as Tay attempted to lift her head but failed.

"I'm calling the cops," she said faintly.

I then snatched the jack hammer from Lorena after she picked it up and finished Tay off. Over and over, I slammed it against her head until her brains resembled red snakes.

I had to think fast, so I took my shirt off and wiped the prints off the weapon and placed it around her car. "Come on, let's put the body in the trunk," I said, making Lorena put a move on.

After the body was in the trunk, I drove it to the middle of the woods and ran back to my car.

Instead of heading to the burger joint, I turned around. We would be heading home. "Listen, I don't think I need to tell you not to mention this to anyone."

"Come on, Judy, I'm not stupid." She sighed and caught her breath. "I didn't mean to hurt her. You believe me, don't you?"

"It doesn't matter. She's dead now and that's the way it had to be." I wouldn't tell anyone either, but I would tell Poppa. He would know what to do. I just felt her body shouldn't have been left in the woods.

When I made it home, Poppa was there with Marty. He came around the corner smiling until he saw me with blood all over me. "Don't move," he said as he turned back down the hall. When he came back, instead of Marty, he had a plastic bag and towels. "What happened? You hurt? I can see this ain't your blood."

"We killed Tay. She was threatening us and Lorena just hit her and I finished it off. I had to, she was going to call the police."

"Take your clothes off. All of them, and wipe what you can

from you then put it all in the bag. Everything will be fine. Where is she?"

"Lorena?"

"No, where is Tay?"

I gave him the directions and he knew exactly what I was speaking of. "She's in the trunk."

"Did you use a phone while out there?"

"No. Not at all."

"Did Lorena?"

"No. I didn't. She didn't either." I realized I was rambling.

"Okay. Everything will be fine. Where's the keys to your car?" I nodded outside. "You left them in the car?"

"Yes, I'm sorry."

"It's cool. Give me the bag and go shower. Don't worry about nothing, I got you. Ight?"

"Okay."

He walked out the door but came back immediately. "You trust Lorena?"

"I do."

"You sure? Let me know now."

"I promise I do." I meant that.

"Bet. Go shower, use bleach under your fingertips. I'll be home later, don't wait up."

"Okay."

After he left, I stood at the door for a minute just staring into space until I heard my son. "Mama."

Before turning to face him, I wiped the tears from my eyes and took a deep breath. "Hey, baby."

"Food."

"Shower first. Okay?"

"Okay."

"Come on. Watch TV while Mommy showers."

"TV!" He clapped his hands. I couldn't hold him so I made him follow me upstairs.

While in the shower, I thought about Liyza and what she would do when she realized Tay wasn't ever coming home again. I knew they would never find her body. A part of me felt sad for my friend, but a huge part of me felt this was what she needed. Maybe not to this extreme, but she definitely needed to be free from Tay.

After showering, I went to the basement to check on Maddy. The moment I stepped off the stairs, it's like she could see right through me.

She lifted herself from the bed and pulled the chains off her waist. "You got blood on your hands." She smirked and then looked worried. "You ain't no better than me now."

Chapter 7
Nadia
Blades of Grass

I t was after midnight and Ayshan hadn't been seen all day today. She said she had to find Maddy before her dad took matters into his own hands. She said she didn't want him to leave what he was doing to come here for someone like Maddy. Not when she could handle it. Hearing her talk like this, knowing I couldn't stop her, hurt me. I hated the fact that she would dirty her soul at such a young age, if at all. As a mother, it was heartbreaking. She did so much to protect her family but never really allowed anyone to protect her. It amazed me how passionate she was. What amazed me just as much was that Chance was showing signs of being just like her sister. Maybe Saw was right when he said my genes were strong. Being the way I was had been embedded in my DNA.

As I watched TV, I got a call from Poppa. This wasn't normal at all. "Hello?" Did he know that I had came over, discreetly searching for Maddy? Did Judy know what I was doing?

"We're going for a ride. Walk to the next block."

"Okay." I asked no questions and got dressed. Poppa was one person I trusted with my entire existence.

"I'm coming," Chance said.

I looked up to her standing at the door with a jacket and shoes on. "What?"

"You're about to go. I want to come too."

"I don't think you should."

"You're about to see him. Aren't you?"

"Who?"

"Ayshan's dad."

I then thought about it. That's why Poppa was outside. He was about to take me to see Saw. "I think so."

"I want to meet him."

"Why?"

"I just want to meet the man who killed my father."

Grabbing my throat, I said, "Honey, don't say that."

"The problem is you think I'm stupid. You underestimate my ability to think outside of an emotional child's level. I know everything."

"Ayshan." I grabbed my forehead.

"I made her tell me. Grandma was praying one night and I heard the prayer when God did."

"What did she say?"

"She asked for God to bless my dad's soul for he was a bad man. She also asked for God to bless Saw's soul for taking my dad's soul."

Hearing my mom's prayer broke my heart. "Your dad almost got—he was—your dad wasn't who you thought he was." I struggled with finding the right words to say.

"I know. I just want to meet the man who took his life away. The man who stopped my dad from killing innocent men."

Sighing, I was starting to realize I didn't have much of a choice. She wasn't going to let me walk out that door without her, so we both walked out.

When we got to the car, Poppa looked confused but still

41

unlocked the back door for her. "What's this? Why is she here?"

"She's met Ayshan. She knows everything."

"Nadia." He took a deep breath and shook his head. "Are you well? Have you lost your fucking mind? Do you understand what's going on?" He drove.

"I promise I won't say anything, Poppa. I've been knowing for months."

"Chance, don't talk," I said. She was already out of place enough. I didn't want her talking to Poppa like she was his equal. She wasn't. She was still a child and soon, I needed to remind her of that. Now I was seeing why Saw didn't want any of this. Now that it was happening, I didn't want it either. It was too much.

We drove down some back roads for a little over an hour until we reached a turn-off point. The trail took us really deep into the woods until we made it to the back edge of the Colorado River. There was a small, wooden house. The next thing I noticed was how bright the moon shined back here without city lights. The last thing I noticed was the boat and an old man at the wheel with Saw at the back, sitting on the dock.

His skin glowed so perfectly in the moonlight. He had on a white shirt with some jeans. On top of his head was a stylish, white turban. When he noticed us walking up, he stood and met me halfway. He first kissed me, then kneeled down to kiss my big belly. "Chance, how are you?" he said.

I turned to around to see Chance shyly coming from behind a tree. "Come here," I said, holding my hand out.

She kept her head down and rushed over to us. "This is Saw, Ayshan's dad."

"Hi, Mr. Saw."

He kneeled down to meet her face. "Please, call me Saw. I

understand you wanted to meet the man who killed your father." I remembered he had cameras on the picture frame.

"Yes."

"I owe you that. Ask me anything you want to know and I promise to be honest."

"Why?"

"He put your mother in danger amongst other things that would've eventually brought everyone around him down." He gently grabbed her face. "I want you to know how sorry I am. If I caused any pain, I deeply apologize. I'll spend the rest of my life making it up to you by protecting you all." Chance shocked me when she started crying and pulled him in for a hug. He rubbed her back. "I know. I know."

"Did he suffer?"

He pulled back and looked into her eyes. "No, he didn't suffer. He didn't make me mad enough to make him suffer. He pissed me off, but he didn't upset me to the point where I wanted to make him suffer."

"Have you ever made anyone suffer?"

"Yes."

"What did they do?"

"Some people can't just be killed. Some I need information from so I have to make them suffer."

"How many people have you killed?"

"I don't know."

"Has my mother ever killed?"

He looked up at me. "You will have to ask her. I'll answer anything about me."

"Do you love her?"

"I'm in love with your mother."

"Then why can't you be with her? My grandmother said you always get my mom pregnant and leave her."

"Your grandmother doesn't know all that she thinks she does."

"Why can't you be with my mother so Ayshan and I can be together and we all be a family?"

He tried not to laugh. "I wish it was that simple. I really wish it was."

"What makes it complicated?"

Poppa chuckled and so did I. "That's enough questions," I said to her.

"Life makes it complicated. You may understand a lot right now, but it's certain things you won't understand until you're older. Can you accept that answer?"

"Yes."

"Chance, let them talk. Come back here with me," Poppa said before she could form another question.

Thank you, I mouthed to him as she walked toward him with her back to me.

"I tried to stop her from coming," he said. "She snuck away. I've taught her well, maybe too well."

"Did you come to drag her home?"

"I did. Can't stay long so I used the little time I did have to see if I could find her, but she's slid below the radar."

"She's tough, huh?"

"Very tough," he agreed. His eyes were glued onto me like they were the nights we made love. Made me miss him and he wasn't gone yet.

"I feel like I'm losing my balance," I found myself saying.

"I won't let you fall."

"Did you get any luck on finding Maddy? I don't think she's with Judy."

"What?" Poppa asked, walking on side of us. "What is she talking about?"

Saw looked as if I had opened my mouth and let the cat out.

"Maddy is back in Austin. We don't know where she is but before she left Haiti, she escaped two attempts."

Poppa massaged his beard and frowned. "She's back *here*? In Texas? In Austin, Texas?"

"Before she left Haiti, she said some dangerous things. Things that could damage us all."

Without saying anything, Poppa walked away to where he was. It was clear that he was highly upset.

"I'm so sorry. I didn't know you didn't tell him."

"Don't worry about it." He dragged his attention back to me. "My wife wants to meet you."

"Here we go."

"She deserves that."

"I didn't cheat on her."

"I know, I did. But a child has came out of this and she wants to be a part of it."

"She wants to be a part of my birth?"

"Yes."

"No. Absolutely fucking not."

"Just think about it."

"Boss man, we gotta go *now*," the boatman said.

Saw turned back to me and kissed my forehead. "Just think about it. Please."

"I'll think about it."

"That's all I want." He headed toward the boat but turned around just before stepping on. "I know Ayshan can take care of herself but please look after her." He paused and caught himself before choking up. "That's my baby girl."

"I will. I promise."

The ride home was long and quiet. Chance was still crying and Poppa said nothing at all. "I'm sorry, I thought you knew," I said as he parked a block over from my home.

"It's cool. Y'all be easy." His jaws clenched.

After we made it in the house, it started to rain. I knew something was wrong when I immediately smelled the rain and heard it clearly like a window was up.

When back in my room, Chance and I were shocked to see Ayshan all bruised up and laying in the middle of the floor crying. I shut the door and ran to her aide. "What happened?" I placed her head on my lap.

"I was way in over my head." She grabbed me and cried harder.

Tears came to my eyes too. To hear her sounding like she had failed in the worst way did something terrible to me. "Talk to me, what happened?"

"I was watching Judy's mother's house, covering all bases looking for Maddy, and a man caught me. He drug me into the woods and beat me. He was about to kill me but a woman caught him and stopped him."

"Did she help you?"

"No. It was Judy's mom. She made him stop."

"What?"

"It was her husband. I'm so confused, Mom. He beat me like he knew me. He told me to tell my dad he said hi."

"What the fuck?" I couldn't stop my heart from pounding. On behalf of my baby, I tried to calm down so I wouldn't stress him out in there.

"Was his name Donnie?" Chance asked, looking nervous.

"Yes, she called him Donnie," Ayshan said, looking confused.

"How you know that, Chance?" I asked.

"Oh my God." She paced back and forth. "I knew it. I knew it. Oh my God."

"What?" I asked. Now I had lost my patience. If she didn't say something soon, I would start screaming and wake everyone up.

"The day Ayshan came to my school, it was career day. Mr. Donnie came since he was on the board of the state and his son goes to my school."

"Keep on. What the hell?" Fuck was she pausing for?

"When Ayshan left, he was walking up to the school. He asked me who that was. I told him I didn't know. He said he knew her dad."

"And you never thought to say anything to me? Or her? Chance?!"

"At the time, I didn't know the severity of what he'd said, Mom. I'm so sorry. I thought nothing of it. I thought he was just making conversation since we were both headed up the steps to the school."

Chapter 8
Judy
Really Did it This Time

I was woken up by Poppa dragging me out of bed and slamming me into the wall. If Marty had slept with us tonight, the slam would've woken him up immediately.

"Baby, what's wrong?" The look of fire in his eyes scared me for dear life. It didn't even look like him anymore.

"Where is she?"

"Who?"

He snatched me from one wall to the next. My head banged against it. "Don't fuck with me, Judy? Where the hell is she?"

"Why would she be here?"

He let me go and attempted to calm down. "I know Maddy. She's desperate. This is the first place she would go because she knows you're fucking weak. Where is she? I'm only asking one more time."

"I don't know, baby, I wouldn't lie to—"

My feet were lifted off the ground and his strong hand had a hard grip on my neck. I couldn't talk or breathe. The more I fought, the more he strangled me. "Are...you...fucking stupid?!" I had never seen him this upset before.

I felt myself losing consciousness right before he easily

lifted me and tossed me into the shower. Cold water slammed down on my face, causing me to scream from shock. "She's in the basement!" Though I was dizzy and disoriented, I followed behind him as fast as I could to the basement. "Poppa, wait," I said as I made it to the stairs. I then lost my balance and tilted over. He turned around and caught me before I fell and tossed me over his shoulder, carrying me with him.

I watched as he stormed into the basement. The minute they saw each other, I felt the tension like it was thick.

He put me down and pulled the gun from the small of his back. Just before he pulled the trigger, she said, "I'm sorry, Poppa! I'm sorry for what happened in Miami! I'm sorry for coming back, but I had to! Someone tried to kill me."

He cocked the gun. "You came back and put my family in danger. Bad shit follows you. I should've killed you but I won't make that mistake again." He rushed over and put the gun in her mouth.

"Wait, I have information," she mumbled the best she could.

"What?" He took the gun out.

"Before coming, I watched Judy but I wasn't the only one."

"Who?"

She described a white man that sounded a lot like my mother's husband. "Give me your phone, Poppa," I said. He handed it to me. I googled Donnie and showed her a picture. "This him?"

"Yes! That's him! That's him! Please don't kill me, I can help. Just trust me, Poppa." When she saw she wasn't getting through to him, she said, "Judy, please."

"Don't say her fucking name! Are you crazy?!" He snatched her up like a child. She looked terrified. She'd never been this scared for her life. Her eyes traveled from me to him. She was scared to even look at me it seemed like. She never let her eyes stay on me longer than a millisecond. After an immense silence, he let her fall onto the bed and headed back up the stairs. "And give her something to change in and clean. It smells like ass." He slammed the basement door.

"Fuck!" I grabbed my neck trying to ease the pain. It didn't matter that I was breaking down in front of Maddy. Fuck Maddy.

"Don't let him kill me. Please."

"Shut up." I ran up the stairs and locked the basement back.

I found Poppa in the room on the phone. "You're calling Saw?"

"I'm sending a signal."

"Who is Donnie?" I asked. "He seemed like a normal guy. Why is he watching me?"

"It's a lot you don't know about Donnie. It's a lot your mother doesn't know about him."

"What business does he have with Saw?"

"Donnie is CIA. He's director of several black sites overseas where he does horrible things to good people."

"Wait, he's not on the board of Texas Repr—"

"It's a cover."

My phone rang. It was Nadia. "Nadia, I have to call you later."

"I need to speak with Poppa."

"Why do you need to speak with him?"

Before she could answer. Poppa snatched the phone from me. "What's up?"

I sat and watched as he went from pissed to outraged. Whatever she was telling him had altered his entire mood. The energy in the room had changed.

"What's wrong?" I asked as he hung up.

"Donnie found Ayshan and assaulted her. He sent a message to Saw."

"He assaulted Ayshan?" I was scared for my mother's life knowing how Saw got down.

"Yes. And your mother saw it happen. She stopped him before he killed Ayshan, but they left her in the woods."

I fell onto the bed, grabbing my chest. "No. Is he going to hurt my mother?" He didn't answer, just looked at me like I was crazy. "Is it going to be right now?"

"No. Not when dealing with Donnie. He can't just walk in like this. But he's definitely on his way back. He's going dark until he kills him. I can't reach him and Ayshan can't either. He's gone dark." Even he looked worried.

"I don't think you should go over your mom's for a while."

"You think Saw would hurt me?"

"This man just tried to kill his daughter and he already has suspicions of you hiding Maddy. This isn't the time to be—do you realize what what the fuck you've done? Huh? Again?" He balled his fist but backed away and punched a hole in the wall. "If I didn't love you, I would've killed you tonight. You know that?"

"But she's chained. It's not like I'm hiding her, baby. Listen to me."

"You still don't get it. After all we've been through with this bitch, you still don't get it. How the fuck don't you get it?" He grabbed my shoulders and shook me like he was trying to shake some sense into me.

"I get it."

"You can't! You can't actually understand. I'm starting to think—" He but himself off and punched another hole in the wall. "Are you stupid? Are you an idiot? What the fuck? How long were you going to keep her down there? Huh? What did you think would happen? How did you think this would go?"

"She just showed up. What was I supposed to do?"

"You were supposed to call me!"

"You should've been here! You knew you left her alive so why the fuck you wasn't here?! This is just as much your fault as it is mine." I was now in his face.

"You really went and caught a body knowing you had Maddy in the basement? Are you trying to see how fast you can get yourself killed? Huh?"

"Poppa..."

"I'm sleeping in the guest bedroom. Don't you go back in that basement. Do you hear me? From now on, you leave all this to me. Do you understand?"

"Yes." I nodded. "I'm sorry."

"Fuck out my face." He left.

"I'm sorry!" I screamed. "I'm sorry!" I broke down on the floor. I really did it this time.

Chapter 9
Judy
See About Me

T he next morning I woke up early to take my son to school. Like Poppa said, I didn't go into the basement at all. There was nothing but trouble down there. He told me to cancel all plans for the day on his schedule but handle the business that I could from home.

As I was doing work at home, Liyza kept calling my phone back to back, complaining about how she hadn't seen or heard from her girl. I told her this was normal, but she was convinced that Tay would never turn her phone off on her. I hung up on her and blocked her number for the day. It was too much to deal with and I'd rather spend my time stressing about the problem at hand and not the problem that was over with.

As I was doing some work, there was a knock at the door. Just like I'd expected, it was Lorena. She's told me, via text, that she'd be by later to bake some cookies, but I knew she wanted to smoke weed and clear her nerves. We hadn't taken on any cases the last couple of weeks and I didn't see it happening anytime soon. At least not while this problem persisted.

As I worked, she watched TV and kept an eye on the cookies. I could see how it was hard for her not to mention what happened. She seemed just as nervous as I was about Maddy and Saw.

"Has Liyza called?" she asked.

"Yes. I had to block her so she wouldn't ruin my day."

"She knows something is wrong?"

"She does."

"I just want you to know how sorry I am for putting you in this situation. I don't know why I did what I did."

"Maybe it wasn't so bad. Liyza doesn't have anyone to ruin her life anymore."

"What if she just finds someone else and repeats?"

"I don't think so. It's always been Tay...always."

"How long did they date?"

"Since forever ago. Liyza has never acted like this with anyone. I'm sure it won't happen again."

"I hope not. Have you talked to your mom?"

Just as I was about to answer, Poppa came bursting through the door. "Just the person I was looking for."

"Me?" Lorena asked, looking confused.

"Yes. Sit down. I need to talk to you." He fixed his eyes on me next. "You too. Come over here."

We both walked over to the couch like kids and sat. "Yes?"

"I know what happened with Tay. Don't worry, I cleared the evidence and the body will never be found."

"I don't know what you mean."

"You can trust him. Trust me," I said.

"Listen, I need a favor from you."

"What's that?"

"The mayor's brother—you know him?"

"Donnie? Of course. Why?"

"Me and a friend are looking for him and as of today, he seemed to have fled."

This was news to me. "What?"

"Yes. Donnie is gone." He turned back to Lorena. "Is it possible that you can find him?"

"Yes."

"You sure?"

"I'm one hundred percent sure, but can I ask what's going on?"

To my surprise, Poppa explained to her exactly what he'd explained to me. He told her enough but not too much. "He did that to a little girl? You sure he was going to kill her?"

"Yes. She wouldn't lie about that. Can you help us? We need to find him and time is winding down."

"Will he be killed?"

"Yes," Poppa answered honestly. "He doesn't know who I am but I know who he is. And I know what he's done."

"What's he done?"

"Are you going to help us find him or no?"

"Yes, of course."

"It has to be today."

She realized that he wanted her to leave now and try to find him. So, she grabbed her keys and purse. "The cookies are done, Judy, just slide them out."

"Okay," I said as she walked out.

Poppa went into the basement before I could even say anything to him. Good thing he did though, my mom called soon as the door closed.

"Yes?"

"Hey, baby. I just wanted to touch bases with you. Haven't really heard from you since that day at dinner. I wanted you to know that I'm sorry and I did deal with her. I want to try again, if that's okay with you."

"I've already told you, Mama, it's fine. You don't have to keep apologizing for that."

"Okay, baby. Another thing, have you seen Donnie? He's been out today and hasn't answered any of my calls."

"Mama?"

"Yes?"

"Why on earth would I know where your husband is?"

She laughed it off. "I'm getting old, chile. I'm sorry. I've been asking everyone. He missed a doctor's appointment today so I'm just asking everybody. I'm sorry."

"It's fine but na, I don't know where that white man is."

"Okay. Thank you, and let me know when we can try dinner again. Okay?" She didn't give a damn about that dinner.

"Okay."

"Okay, love you. Bye, bye."

"Love you too." I hung up.

Though I didn't want my mother dead, I hadn't had much to say to her since I found out what she'd done. I couldn't believe she left a child to die.

"What's wrong?" Poppa asked.

"Didn't even notice you were back up here."

"You okay?"

"I think my mother just lied to me."

Chapter 10
Lorena
We Meet Again

I went to the office of the mayor and he wasn't there. Also went to his home, he wasn't there either. The only place I could think of him being was at his second home. The cabin he used for his extramarital affairs. The home I'm sure my son was conceived in. It was just over an hour away, deep, deep in the woods. Though the area was beautiful, I'd always felt like it was perfect for a serial killer. The very first time he brought me here, I thought I would never make it out. Come to find out, he was just a sex addict.

First thing I saw when I pulled in was his personal car. He never drove his personal car places, not really. He was always escorted. Donnie was definitely here

Using my key, I let myself in. My child's father stood right in the living room with the look of complete shock on his face. He looked around like he was expecting someone else to walk through the door. "Lorena? What are you doing here?"

"Where's Donnie?"

"I don't know what you mean."

"Where is he? Don't fucking play with me. I know what he did to that little girl. You're really going to hide him?"

"I have no idea what you're—"

"It's okay, you can tell her." Donnie came walking from around the corner from the kitchen.

"Why did you do that to that little girl?"

"You need to sit for this."

"I'll stand," I said.

"Please? I want to explain things from my point of view and save your life in the process."

"My life?"

"Yes, *your life.*"

"What do I have to do with any of this?" I asked, confused.

"You're friends with a woman named Judy. She's my wife's daughter. A couple of months back, I tracked Judy to a very dangerous man. His name is Abraham." He reached into his pocket and pulled out a phone, showing me a picture of Saw, but with much less hair. He saw the look on my face and nodded. "You've seen this man before. Haven't you?"

"Yes."

"Your life is in danger if you've ever seen this man's face. He's going to track you to my brother, if he hasn't already, and then to me."

"He already has and I'm alive."

He chuckled and stepped back. My baby father sat on the couch and rested his face into his palms. "You have no idea who *Saw* is, do you? What have they told you about him?"

"He's a nice guy."

"That's all you know? Right? They've never went into detail about who he really is, have they?"

"No," I said as I thought back. They never chose to be specific when describing him. It was always surface-level things. Literally all I knew was that his name was Saw, and that wasn't his name.

"Judy's your friend. Right?"

"Right." I thought about Saw some more. There was always

something so mysterious about him and that's a part of what made him attractive to me.

"He's a terrorist who's murdered many, many people."

I swallowed the lump in my throat. "Terrorist?"

"That's a little extreme, isn't it, Donnie?" my baby's father said.

"You may not know, but I work for the CIA and am a director over many black sites."

"Black sites?" I didn't think those type of things were real. Only in movies.

"It takes a lot to defend this country. I'm the man who does the dirty work. I'm the man who does things that people frown upon. A lot of soft people want us to give in to everyone else but if we did, we'd be overthrown in a heartbeat like Ukraine. It takes tough people to make tough decisions. I've done what I had to do!"

"You were seconds away from killing a little girl. A little girl!"

"She's a terrorist in the making! I was doing the world a favor."

"*Saw* did what he had to do also, if that's the case."

"You still don't get it."

"Get what?"

He rushed to my face and my baby father rushed in front of him. "Anyone who's not a friend of the United fucking States is an enemy and must be persecuted."

"What grudges is he holding against you?" I wanted to know.

"That information is classified. The important thing is I've done what I needed to do. He did what he wanted to do and that's the difference."

"Bullshit."

"All of them are going down. All of them. You can either

die trying to protect people that would kill you in a heartbeat or you can protect yourself and my nephew."

"You leave my son out of this, Donnie," my baby's father said, now giving him a death stare.

"She needs to know the truth," he said, now gazing back at me. "We've been looking for Abraham for a long time and God landed him right on my door step."

"He won't have a fair trial and you know it."

"Trial?" Donnie laughed loudly. "Oh no, he won't make it to trial. According to America, he doesn't exist anymore. He just poofed," he spread his fingers, "and vanished into thin air."

"So what? Let him go."

"We will. We're going to let him go to hell. And if you don't want to go with them, you'd mind your fucking business and lead me to him. Or I swear to God, I will take you down with him."

My baby's father was now looking Donnie up and down like he'd lost his mind. "You really need to choose your words correctly, Donnie. I don't want to have to tell you that again."

"Are you with him on this?" I asked my baby's father.

"I don't agree with him but I will keep my brother safe." He shot a mean glance to his brother. "I will also keep my son's mother safe."

"Does your wife know about your son yet? He's so handsome." He winked. "It's the right thing to do. Since we want to blame me for being a bad guy and doing the wrong thing."

"Donnie! Enough!" my baby's father yelled, now standing up to his brother.

Donnie looked over his brother's shoulders and continued talking to me. "Use your common sense, Lorena. Just like my brother is going to protect me, those *people* will protect their family—that terrorist. See, you and my brother have a child so he has to protect both of us, but what's holding you to them?

60

Huh? A friendship with Judy? The poor little adopted girl. Come on." He sighed and snapped his fingers. "I still don't know the full connection Judy has to *Saw*. I've connected her to Nadia and Nadia to some footage of her with a little girl who I'm pretty sure belongs to her and *Saw*. But I still can't find what connected Judy. Maybe you can help me with that. How does she know them?"

That's when I remembered Judy's baby father who wasn't living with her a couple of months ago. It surprised me that his wife hadn't told him, being that she'd met Poppa a few times. That's when it hit me, he didn't know who Poppa was at all. He still hadn't connected Poppa to Haiti, which would've connected him to Nadia and Saw.

"I don't know."

"I think you do," he said.

Right then and there, I saw what needed to be done. There was no escaping a catastrophic outcome. "How fast can you have me out of the state?"

"Immediately," he said.

"I need to get my son from school right now. I'm sure he's looking for you, too. It's why I'm here. I'm going to tell them I didn't find you."

"Do you know where he is?" Donnie asked.

"No, but I'm sure I can find him."

My baby's father neared me and gently grabbed my shoulders. "Take our son and go somewhere far away. Don't go to your hometown. Don't even tell me where you are until I call and tell you it's all over. Okay?"

I nodded. "Okay."

"Pick our son up and find out where Abraham is. Okay? Move quickly."

"Okay."

"I love you," he said as he led me to the front door.

Tears left my eyes as I drove away and called my son's school, telling them to have him ready. I then called Judy. "Lorena? Everything okay?" she wanted to know.

"There's been a change of plans and I want to apologize now before I tell you."

Chapter 11
Judy
Blood and Back Stabbing

G oing behind Poppa's back, I went to pick my mother up after I got the call from Lorena. First thing I told her was that I knew where her husband was and I would take her to him. It didn't go unnoticed when she failed to ask me how I suddenly knew where he was. She willingly jumped in the car. Her only question to me was asking about his safety.

Not even when I turned down the heavily wooded area did she question me. That's when I knew that my mother knew way more than what she let on. I was willing to bet that at this point, she knew who Saw was.

When we got to the nice cabin, Donnie and the mayor looked utterly confused but more so upset. "Donnie! You're safe." My mother ran to him, kissing him. He never took his eyes off me.

"She called you. Didn't she?" Donnie asked.

"Who?" my mother asked, turning around.

"Lorena," I said, not taking my eyes off either of them.

"Who's Lorena?"

"It's how I fully connected the dots. I've been telling you about Abraham," he said to her. "They call him Saw."

"What did she tell you?" my mother asked me.

"Lorena? The girl you *didn't know* just a minute ago?"

"Yes." Her entire attitude changed. She got so cold. "I won't let Donnie hurt you, but you have to tell me where Abraham is."

"Like you let him hurt that little girl?"

"She lived."

"She has a broken nose."

"She lived," she said again.

"He almost killed her."

"But he didn't. Besides, she'd been watching us."

"You're repulsive, you and him."

"Where is Saw, Judy?" She wasn't even calling me cute little pet names anymore. My how things changed.

"I don't know. I came here to save myself. Lorena wanted me to flee with her but obviously, I can't. I'm in too deep. So, I came to make a deal with the devil."

"Judy, you can wait until personnel is called in before you do this," the mayor said nervously. "I want to make sure you're safe after you're no longer valuable."

His harsh truth hurt bad, but it opened my eyes to something—he was afraid his mother would kill me once I told him where to find Saw. "Nobody has been called in yet?"

"No," the mayor said.

Something was off right now. Something was really off. "Mom, please don't tell my siblings. Wanda already hates me. Camille sees the best in me right now."

"I haven't told them or anyone else anything. You have my word."

"What will happen to my son?"

"Donnie and I will keep him. You'll do two years at the least."

She'd just lied to me again. Nobody, and I do mean nobody,

ever got two years when dealing with terrorists. That's when I started to play with an intrusive thought. "Mom?"

"Yes?"

"You work with the CIA too, don't you?"

She glanced at her husband. He nodded, giving her permission to talk to me. "Yes, I do. They gave me a family, picking me right from the adoption agency. Right after I gave birth to you."

"Wow. How long have you known about my connection to Saw?"

"For a couple of months."

She never mentioned Marcel and that was awkward. "What about Marcel?"

"What about him?" she asked. "Nadia is *your friend*. You're the one with the connection to Saw, not Marcel. He's not even living under the same roof as you."

There it was, she didn't know. She truly had no idea who Marcel was. He'd succeeded in hiding his true self from her and rightfully so. "Mom?"

"Yes?"

"Where's Marcel from?"

"Well, he's from Florida."

I had all the information I needed. Nobody had been called yet. I pulled out my phone and called Poppa. "It's time."

"What's going on?" My mother and Donnie seemed to have panicked, but I noticed the mayor seemed eerily calm right now. I couldn't figure it out.

When Lorena called me, she told me it would be a change of plans and apologized. She said she wasn't sure but she had feelings that my mom was in on all of this. She said I had to make a tough decision today. I would have to choose my family that Poppa gave me or my mother, who I was just meeting for the first time. She gave me the location and told me to give it to Poppa and Saw also.

I told her I didn't feel comfortable being there at the cabin alone, but she told me I wouldn't be alone. I didn't know what she meant.

Donnie tried to make a call but his cellular didn't seem to be dialing out. My mother then tried to make a call and hers also didn't work. That meant Saw was close by now. He'd jammed the services.

I tried to make another call to be sure, and mine didn't dial out either. While they panicked, I felt relieved. I was just ready for all this to be over for good. I was so tired of blood and back stabbing.

"Who else have you told?" the mayor asked Donnie.

"I've told nobody yet. You snatched me from my home so fast that I didn't have time to call anyone." Then Donnie seemed to have made a shocking discovery. "How did you know?"

"Know what?" the mayor asked.

"I never told you anything that was going on until we got to this cabin, but somehow you knew to come and pick me up." Donnie moved swiftly but not fast enough. Before he could reach for his gun, the mayor had already shot him point blank between the eyes.

"Donnie!" my mother yelled, rushing to his aid, but the mayor stopped her.

"Get on the ground, Cat."

Cat? My mother's nickname was Cat? What an odd way to find out.

She stood still, looking all around as if she was looking for a weapon or way out. "Caaaat," he said, as if he was talking to a child, telling them not to do something. "The ground."

She dropped to her knees, and in walked Saw and Poppa. My mother's mouth dropped to the ground. "Marcel?"

"Why didn't you stop this? Huh? After all I've done for

you?! The only thing I asked was that you keep him under control. That was the deal so I wouldn't kill him. Right?" Saw said to the mayor as he rushed toward him, but the mayor didn't stand down.

"I didn't know he was still looking into you. He hadn't mentioned it to me in years. And how the fuck was I supposed to know your daughter was here? You didn't tell me! I wasn't in the loop!" Saw stepped back and made sense of what the mayor was saying. They both put their weapons away. "I haven't gotten a signal from you in a while besides today."

"Is he dead?" Saw asked.

The mayor dropped to his knees and checked Donnie's pulse. "Yes."

Poppa was right, underestimating Saw would be a grave mistake for anyone to make. He really had friends in high places.

A mayor had just murdered his brother because of Saw. He clearly owed him a huge favor. It made me wonder how high Saw's connections reached. Right now I was looking at him in a brand-new light. Saw was dangerous in every which way.

Poppa never needed Lorena for anything. Not even to find Donnie. They knew where Donnie was this entire time. He was testing her loyalty to see if she would take the offer he knew Donnie would make. She didn't, she gave Donnie up instead. It felt good to know that I had a friend this time, a real friend.

"Let me go, baby girl. Please. I'm your mother. You hear me? We can work this out. Just tell them to let your mama go."

She was calling me cute pet names again. "How do I know you're not going to betray everyone in this room the minute I let you go?"

Saw lifted his gun, but Poppa placed his hand over it, lowering it back down. He was going to allow me to make this tough decision. "I wouldn't do that to you, baby. You're my daughter. You're my baby girl. I wouldn't harm you."

Blinking tears away, I nodded up at the mayor, who was now right behind my mother with his weapon pointed to the back of her head. "No! No!" she cried as I walked away.

Pop!

The bullet sounded so loud. Way louder than Donnie's death bullet. I knew it seemed that way because of the emotional attachment to my mother. "The maids are already on the way to clean this up," I heard Poppa say.

I felt like a zombie when I opened the door and the sunlight hit me hard. Sunshine seemed so different now. My entire perspective had changed. Things were different now. This time was different than last time, way different.

When I got home, Lorena was in her car waiting. When I told her about everything, even she was shocked that the mayor and Saw had ties from years back. She said he never mentioned it. She thought he wanted her to flee for real. I'm so glad she didn't.

Chapter 12
Judy
Back in One Peace

Two months later...

My mother's body was never found. Neither was her husband's. Yet and still, they chose to have a funeral. The media sold the narrative that my mother and Donnie went on a trip and never returned. I knew the mayor played a huge part in that being that he said his last conversation with his brother was telling him that he and the wife were taking a much-needed trip. He had Donnie's phone so it wasn't hard for him to put the text on his phone.

I hated what this had done to Camille. She wasn't the same anymore. She'd even broken up with her boyfriend and chose to raise our little brother.

Wanda had become more bitter than before and the other brother moved out of state with his wife. They sold the house and gave the money to Camille since she was the one who took in our teen brother.

Of course, I gave my condolences, but Wanda still held a grudge against me for being born.

Maddy was taken care of but for good this time. Saw made sure of that. He left no room for error so he did it himself.

Liyza had finally decided to go to rehab when she realized Tay wasn't coming back. That's where Lorena and I were on the way to right now—to visit Liyza at the rehabilitation center just outside of Austin. It was a beautiful, lakeside community with a farm. To keep them busy, there were plenty of activities, including tending to the animals. Most of the residents chose to tend to the farm animals. The other half spent time cooking the edible farm animals.

After we checked in, we grabbed a seat and some of the good food they served. Liyza came out with the biggest smile on her face. She was glowing these days. Lorena and I nodded at each other in approval at the new Liyza. See, this Liyza was new to Lorena but this was the Liyza I'd known before Tay.

"Finally, you hoes decide to come," Liyza said, snatching a cupcake from Lorena's plate.

"We just came two weeks ago," I said.

"Two weeks is a long time."

"So how's everything?" Lorena asked. By the sneaky look on Liyza's face, I knew she was about to say some bullshit.

"I had sex."

"What's new? Who's the girl?" I asked.

She leaned in. "It wasn't a girl."

"What?" Lorena and I asked in unison.

"Shhh, keep y'all voice down."

"Who?"

"Please don't tell me he was a resident?" I asked. That's all we needed was for her to fall in love with another addict.

"No, it was Mellow."

"Mellow!" I said.

"Shhh!"

"The one who used to work here?" Lorena asked, leaning in closely.

"Yes."

"Chile, he cute but ain't he a lil' too much...man for you?" Lorena said. I was wondering the same thing. Mellow was a big, tall, and thick man. One day we saw his dick print at a visit and stared at it the entire time. It was huge.

"I'm saying. Have you ever even had dick in your adult life?" I asked.

"Nope." She'd been molested as a child but in her adult life she steered clear of dick.

"How it feel?" I wanted to know.

"It hurt at first but—"

"Ahh, this hoe a punk bitch," Lorena cut her off.

"Like I said," Liyza continued, "it hurt at first but it eventually started to feel good. I can't believe I been missing out on dick. He was so gentle with me." She blushed like a little child.

We continued to laugh with Liyza until time was up. While on the way home, I got a call from Nadia telling me she'd had her son during an at-home water birth. She'd told me she wanted to do it at home but I didn't believe she would go through with it.

"She had the baby," I said to Lorena.

"Nadia?"

"Yea."

"Did Saw allow his wife to come? Well, did Nadia allow it?"

"I think so."

"She better than me, I know that much."

"Me too."

"Why she want to be there anyway? I don't see why Saw just won't take Nadia overseas and marry them both."

"She wouldn't go for that."

"She might," Lorena said, shrugging her shoulders. After some time passed by, she sighed and said, "So, I'm dating again."

"That's good. Who?"

"It's a guy in Dallas. Your baby daddy introduced us."

"Wait, huh?"

"Yea. Remember that property I took him to see last month?"

"Yea."

"Well, a man met him there. He said it was an old friend of his."

"What was his name?"

"Felipe."

"He's Hispanic?"

"His father is. He's so fine. No, he's *foine*," she said, blushing how Liyza was just blushing.

"Never heard of him. Maybe that's why Poppa keeps telling me he wanted to visit Dallas one of these weekends."

"Maybe so."

"Does your baby father know?"

"He does and you know what? He's okay with me dating now. We're in a good place."

"I'm glad to hear that."

"We had sex for the first time last night."

"For real?" It was crazy to me that she was finally ducking off with anyone other than the mayor.

"Yes. It was so good. He wants me to move with him but I told him we needed more time. My baby daddy ain't going for that."

"You know he not."

"It still feels so good to just be wanted by someone else again. You know?"

"I know the feeling."

Chapter 13
Nadia
Extended Family

Chance and Ayshan cleaned the tub area of everything as I held my healthy baby boy. My mother and two other kids had gone to Haiti to visit family, thinking they were getting it out the way before the baby came, but he ended up coming a weekend earlier. It sucked they couldn't be here but I was making the best out of it. Of course, Chance chose to stay with me. She couldn't care less about the family we had in Haiti or any friends there.

Ayshan had just made it as I was pushing him out. She or her dad said they wouldn't miss it for the world.

Saw hadn't made it yet. He and Ayshan used different means of transportation to get here so she arrived before him.

"Did his ride decide to come?" I asked Ayshan.

"Yes. We told her you said she could and she definitely chose to come."

"That's good," I lied. I told him she could come, hoping she would use her common sense and say no. But she was coming anyway. Who in their right mind would want to watch their husband's love child be born?

"Give her a chance, Mom," Ayshan said, reading my facial expressions.

"I am, it's just that, I don't want to deal with all the questions she may have."

"Dad answered them all months ago."

"You sure?"

"I'm sure."

The doula finished cleaning me up and my baby. She didn't leave right away since I asked her to stay and monitor us. She was from Haiti like me so she used some of the same birth rituals.

After a few hours of loving on my beautiful son, Saw and his wife arrived. When she made it in the house, she asked Saw permission to remove her hijab. Once she slid it off, I saw the most beautiful woman I'd seen in a while. She was all natural and looked so pure, clean, and gorgeous. She had big brown eyes like Saw and long, coal-black hair.

She kneeled on side of me, grabbing my hand and kissing it. "Thank you."

"For what?"

"For allowing me into your home, around your son."

"Oh wow. No, it's no problem."

Saw came over and held his arms out. "May I hold him?"

"Of course." I handed our son over. "His name is Aaqil."

"I remember you telling me you would name him that. Glad you stuck to it."

"What a beautiful name," Saw's wife said. "Back home, they call me Khadijah."

"Thank you, Khadijah." She raised from her knees and stood next to Saw as they admired my son. As I watched her eyes fill with love, all I could think about was how she felt the first time she met Ayshan. I imagined she looked at her the same way. There was no indifference or prejudice shown with her and I appreciated it. It actually warmed my heart. "You can hold him if you want," I said to her.

"Oh, thank you, thank you."

Saw winked at me and gently placed our son into her arms. She smelled him immediately. "I love the smell of babies."

"I understand you had one months ago?"

"Yes. Our children are home with my parents."

"Why didn't you bring them?" I asked her.

She giggled. "Nooooo. Too many."

"I understand."

Ayshan came and walked Khadijah away with the baby to give Saw and I some alone time.

He closed the door and sat next to where I laid on the bed. His hand then rubbed my leg. "You did great. He's healthy and beautiful."

"Thank you."

"Thanks for taking my advice and also having him home like you did with Ayshan."

"No problem. A water birth was actually a game changer for pain."

"I bet it was. You look so beautiful."

"Thank you." I could tell there was something he wanted to say but couldn't. "What?"

"I was thinking, maybe you should come with me for a while overseas."

"What?"

"Hear me out. We both were young when Ayshan was born so we were forced to live apart. I want to raise our son together."

"With me and your other family? What about my other children?"

"My place has more than enough space for everyone. You think I would ask you to leave your other kids here? Never."

"What about Mom?"

"Her too. She's family."

"Saw, no. Hell no." I thought about it and said, "hell no," again. "Ayshan said y'all don't eat junk food and everyone does their part on the farm."

"What's wrong with that?"

"I don't want to live like that. My kids aren't used to that kind of life."

"Okay, so I buy you your own place and you'd still marry me."

"Marry you?" I asked. I couldn't have heard him right.

"Yes. I talked to my wife and she's fine with me exercising my right to more than one wife."

"Saw, I don't—I don't know...I can't."

"It's beautiful in my country. It's far better than Haiti. The news only shows you a war and rubble, but I wouldn't raise my kids there if it was as bad as they made it seem."

"I can't."

"Why not, my Nadia? What's keeping you here?"

"I can't share you with another woman." My voice cracked. "I can't."

"So you want our son to grow up like Ayshan did? She didn't know the other parent."

"My other kids have a dead father, so what's the difference?"

"They got to meet him. They knew him. Our son deserves that. Or at least..."

"At least what?"

"I don't want to be a part from him. I love all of my children so much and he's no different."

"So what are you asking?"

"If you won't come, at least let's try splitting his time with me and here in America with you."

"That's going to be different."

"At least he will be well versed in both cultures."

"This is a lot to ask." My heart sank. I didn't think this deep into it when I gave birth. It was all settling in now—my son would come up like Ayshan did. I had a choice but I didn't like the choice.

"Do you love me?" he asked, grabbing my chin.

"You know I do."

"Then work with me, my Nadia."

"I can't possibly make that decision today."

"I know. I'm not asking you to, not right now. But I do want you to make it soon. Maybe after you heal?" I was still a bit speechless. "I'll give you the world. Anything you want. Just please."

"Do you want me or your son?"

"I want you and *our* son. I love you so much and I just don't want this to happen again. My family can be a big help to you and your other children. It's so beautiful in my country."

"I'll think about it," I said. "I promise."

Chapter 14
Lorena
For Moral Support

T he day after Nadia had the baby, Judy's sister, Camille, held a dinner and invited Judy. Since the dinner would be held at her home, she wanted to try again at what their mother failed to do—hold a dinner with all the kids.

Judy was going to go alone but I suggested she take me for moral support. Or to have her back in case someone got out of line. I didn't want anyone to try and gang up on her. It wouldn't happen, at least not successfully, with me in attendance.

As we sat at the table, Wanda never took her eyes off Judy and I never took my eyes off her. Camille had just finished giving a speech about family and sticking together, but Wanda seemed to not have heard shit she said. Not with the death stare she was giving Judy.

The youngest brother, Michael, had become very fond of Judy and fast. Jason liked Judy but it was obvious he wanted to hold up his loyalty to Wanda. They both looked predominantly white. It figured that the kids who looked black *and* white— Camille and Michael—had a great relationship with Judy. They'd actually gotten closer since their father had been gone.

Nobody really had anything good to say about Donnie but Wanda and Jason. Go figure again.

"Can you pass me the chicken?" Judy asked Michael.

"I bet you love fried chicken," Wanda said. Her husband shook his head and continued eating.

"I do. What do you like? Donald Trump?" Judy shot back.

That must have stung Wanda hard because she almost slapped her man for laughing. "Are we even sure she's our sister?"

"Wanda, I'm warning you. I'm nothing like Mom. I will not tolerate this," Camille said, eating mashed potatoes. "I love your hair, Judy. It's so nice and big. I wish I could get my hair to stay like that," Camille said, trying to sift over her other ugly ass sister's racist comments.

I had never in life seen anything like this. Not even close. Wanda really was sitting at this table being racist with people who shared her bloodline. She seemed proud of herself.

"Thanks. I love your hair also."

Wanda laughed and covered her mouth. "Jason, I love your hair," she said.

He laughed, knowing that joke wasn't funny.

Michael, the youngest brother, said, "Can we act like adults at this table?"

"And that's a teenager telling you this," Camille said.

"What does he know about maturity? He spends every free hour playing a video game where they kill people and fuck prostitutes in the ally," Wanda said.

"Oh fuck you, Wanda."

"Don't use that language," Jason said.

"Fuck you too. You only speak up to condone the shit Wanda does. Suck my dick." He stormed away from the table.

"That was real mature," Wanda said.

"Wanda..." Camille said in a tone that told me she was

losing her patience.

"I don't see how you fuck her at night with a soul so ugly like that," I said to Wanda's husband. See, I knew how to piss a bitch off.

"Excuse me?" Wanda asked. "And who the fuck are you?"

"Someone that's had it with your bullshit. Are you upset that Judy was born or that she's all black?"

"My mother was black. How dare you call me a racist. Get out!"

I stood and grabbed my purse. "Sit down, Lorena. Please," Camille said calmly.

"Camille?" Wanda sounded apprehensive and appalled.

"What?"

"I told her to get out."

"This isn't your house."

"Either they leave or me and my family leaves."

"Goodbye."

Wanda wasted no time grabbing her wine glass and tossing the rest of it onto me.

I don't remember how or when I got to her, but it happened quickly. By the time I was pulled off of her, her fake lashes and tracks that weren't glued in right were all the way in the kitchen. Wanda's face was black and blue. She threatened to call the cops but I wasn't worried. My baby's father would have those charges dropped instantaneously.

Luckily, Jason talked her out of it and she opted to leave instead. Jason and his woman left with them, leaving me, Camille, and Judy at the table.

"Welp," Camille said, lifting her wine glass for a toast. "That was an epic failure."

We all laughed and tapped glasses. We drank more wine and ate more food. The night turned out to be a hot mess but we loved it.

Chapter 15
Judy
I Can Do This All Day

I got home after midnight, drunk and feeling good. Poppa had already put Marty in bed as he laid on the couch with his hand behind his head. I started to go straight for the shower, but I decided to plop onto him instead.

"Drunk ass. How you get home?"

"Lorena. Duh." I stretched out even more onto his lap.

He rubbed my ass and continued watching TV. I was too drunk to open my eyes and see what he'd been watching but it sounded like cartoons. "Poppa? Baby?"

"What's up?"

"Lorena just beat the shit out of Wanda."

"Gone on." He laughed.

I turned onto my back, looking up at him. "She did. So much for us getting along now."

"Do you want a relationship with Wanda?"

"Not really. She's a shitty person."

"Well then, don't worry about her."

"Am I wrong for getting satisfaction from her getting her ass beat?"

"I don't think so. It's not your fault she can't hold her own."

"Yea, you so right. Fuck her."

"You ready for bed?"

"No. I want to lay on you." I smelled my armpits. "I stink? I don't stink."

"Na, baby. You don't stink." I couldn't tell if he was lying to me or not.

"Baby?"

"What's up?"

"You mean so much to me."

"You mean so much to me more."

"Was that even a sentence?"

"You drunk. Your ass wasn't supposed to peep that." He leaned down and kissed me.

"Baby?"

"What's up?"

"You mad at me?"

"About what?"

"The situation with Maddy."

"Na. You're just a good person, Judy. I can't fault you for that. It's one of the main things that made me love you."

"I thought it was this wet pussy."

"That too."

"Umhmm."

"Come on, let's go shower."

"Nooooo."

"Yea, come on." He picked me up with ease and carried me like a newborn child. As he walked us up the stairs, the moon shined onto his face. He stared down at me with so much compassion. "Judy, you crying?" he asked.

"Remembering the night I met you. What if I wouldn't have ever taken the trip? I almost turned around. Then I wouldn't have ever met you."

"Don't think about that."

"Why not?"

"Because we met so that's not our story."

"In another universe, another me didn't meet you and she's sad."

He laughed.

We made it to the bedroom. With me still in his arms, he reached down and ran me some bath water. He then helped me undress and placed me into the warm water. "You put lavender in here. Yay."

"Just like you like." He tilted my head back and wet it.

"My hair!"

"You got wine in it. Did Lorena fight or you?"

"Wanda tossed the wine and some of it got in my hair, I guess."

"Your drunk ass just chilling, not even knowing."

"Not even caring," I corrected. I sighed and completely relaxed.

"You're so beautiful."

"You're just saying that to get me out this tub so you can sleep."

"I can do this with you all day, pretty girl."

"Awww, baby."

"I can. You so beautiful to me. Never seen nothing like you."

"Now that she's gone, like really gone, do you ever miss her?"

"Who?"

"The girl."

"Who?" he asked, confused.

"Maddy."

"Na, pretty girl. I'm actually relieved. She was causing too many problems. I wanted her to live because I did love her way back then, but she was always going to be a threat to you as long as she lived."

"I'm built Ford tough."

"In a way like a toy truck would be."

"Oh please."

"I'm about to start nutting in you again. Every single day."

"What? Why?"

"I want you to have my baby."

"I have your baby."

"Another baby." He looked so serious and focused on me still.

"What I'ma do with two kids?" I said, mocking Ike Turner.

"You so silly. *What's Love Got to Do With It*, right? Ain't that the movie?"

"Right."

"You funny. We can do a lot with two kids. I want more than two."

"Three?"

"Seven."

"Ten? My vagina..."

"I'm kidding." He gave me a side eye. "Buuuuut, maybe I'm not."

"Why seven?"

"I don't know. I just like that number. We can have more."

"More?"

"Yea. My gran got so many kids that even *she* lost count. If you ask her how many kids she got, she got to call them by name and add them up. Then she get them confused. It's written down somewhere."

"How many she got?"

"I thought it was like thirteen at first until I got to thinking about it one day. Gran didn't stop having children until she was in her early fifties."

"Fifties?!"

"I know, huh?"

"Wow. That's amazing. I still don't like her."

"Leave my gran alone."

"No, she need to leave me alone."

"She's old."

"So what? That gives her an excuse to be evil to me?"

"I don't believe she knows she's being evil. It's just that for so long, everyone just accepted her because she was *Gran*. She has grandchildren that she can't stand and she tells them every chance she gets."

"See? Evil."

"You don't have to deal with her anymore."

"I know, but that don't take away the fact that she's pure evil."

"You doing too much now. She ain't pure evil."

"I'm sorry."

"You good. Ready to get out?"

"Yep." He grabbed a towel and wrapped me up in it. "Pajamas?"

"What you need those for?"

I smirked. "I'm ovulating."

"How you know?"

"Because I been thinking about your dick since I woke up."

"Say less." He removed his briefs and pushed me onto the bed. He felt how wet I was and kissed me. "Yea, you getting all this dick tonight."

"I want it all night." I spread my legs and let him in.

"I'ma give it to you just like that then—all night."

85

Chapter 16
Judy
...But it's Beautiful

" I should've made a bet with you. I knew it! I fucking knew it!" Lorena said loudly over the phone. She couldn't wait to tell me she told me so.

"Whatever."

"The crazy bitch actually did it. She really moved her family to Iraq to be with Saw...*and his other family.*"

"I can't believe her." It had been three weeks since she'd been gone and I still couldn't believe she actually made the decision to move her mother and kids to Iraq. Though she told me how beautiful it was, it was still crazy for me to believe. Iraq though? Really?

"If she likes it, I love it. Shid, she told me the water was beautiful. What part of Iraq? Like what city?"

I chuckled. "You do know Iraq is definitely a country, right?"

"Yea. Duh."

"Shut up, bitch, you didn't know that."

"So what?"

"It's several places in Iraq, not just one."

"I guess it doesn't matter anyway since he's moving them all to Dubai," she said, reminding me.

"Oh, yea. I forgot he was doing that. All because Nadia suggested it."

"I know that Khadijah was mad as hell."

"Nadia said Khadijah was more excited than her about moving there."

"Dubai is definitely for the rich."

"Saw is very rich and very connected," I said, thinking back on the day he and the mayor revealed themselves to be friends. Old friends at that."

"Whatever. You ready to go out?"

"Yep. Got my dress ready. All you need to do is hang up the phone."

Liyza had been awarded one weekend to come home to visit, and we took advantage by taking her out. We would have drinks but Liyza said she didn't want any drinks.

"Bye."

We hung up and got dressed.

When we made it to the high-end restaurant near downtown, I expected to see many people but only saw Liyza and Lorena.

"Where is everyone?" I asked. The waiter held the door open.

Once inside, I jumped at the large crowd that jumped up and screamed, "Surprise!"

"Happy birthday, girl." Liyza leaned over and kissed me on the cheek. She had on a dress and heels, standing next to Mellow.

"Don't cry," Lorena said as she rubbed my back.

Nadia was here with her kids and the baby. Saw, Ayshan, and Khadijah were also in attendance. All of the old house workers and their families were there. Even Gran was there with a large group of people surrounding her.

Nadia rushed over to me, patting her baby. "Those people

with Gran are all of Poppa's family back in Haiti. All Gran's kids, grandkids, and great-grandchildren and so on. Poppa's cousins are even in attendance."

"Good looking out," I said, wiping the tears from my eyes.

"I'm saying. I was like, who the hell is all these people?" Lorena joked. Her man, Felipe, was even there, and he was just as fine as she said he was.

Gran had Marty in her arms, not paying attention to anything else around her. I still couldn't stand her even with the feeling of joy running through me.

Camille and my youngest brother were there too.

"I can't believe you hoes kept this from me," I said to my crew, Nadia, Lorena, Liyza.

"This isn't even the best part," Lorena said, but Nadia hit her shoulder.

"Shut up," she said to her.

"My bad."

"What?" I asked.

Liyza nodded behind me. "Turn around."

I turned around and my heart couldn't dropped right out of my dress. Marcel was right there on one knee with an expensive suit on and an even bigger ring than last time in his hand.

"Shut y'all assed up!" Lorena yelled at the chattering crowd.

"Y'all gone miss the damn proposal," Nadia said, pulling out her phone. Ayshan came and grabbed Aaqil to help her mom out.

Chance stood behind her mom with tears in her eyes. She was so emotional. I loved that about her. When I saw that Gran still hadn't looked up, it pissed me off briefly. Her family even tried to get her attention and point at Poppa. She purposely acted like she was too busy with Marty.

I was about to tell Chance to go and get my damn son, but

Poppa's voice in the sudden silence caught my attention. "Judy, I have loved you since the first moment I saw you in the train station."

"Huh?" me and my crew said in unison.

Saw walked over in his suit, laughing. He then handed Poppa a piece of paper. "Oh, wrong Google proposal. Hold on," Poppa said.

Everyone erupted in laughter. Saw had his hand on Poppa's shoulder like a proud friend of a play boy who was finally settling down.

Poppa then got serious. "Judy, I have loved you since day one. The minute I saw you, I knew I wanted you to be in my life forever. You don't know how happy I was when you called me and told me you were pregnant. I had already been thinking of you, but learning about our son made me love you even more. I would come to your job and watch you. I would ask people what you ate on your lunch break. I had my men sitting outside your house at night to make sure nothing happened to you. You never knew none of this." He choked up.

"Take your time," Saw said, patting his back.

"We've been through so much and you never left my side. I've changed your life in so many ways and not all good, but you stayed. You never even thought about leaving me. You knew you wanted this to work out. You taught me what love was and you ain't even know. You taught me patience. Because I damn sure needed it dealing with you."

Everyone laughed again. Lorena was crying her eyes out and so were Nadia and Liyza. Even Ayshan.

Not Gran, though. *Bitch.*

"I guess what I'm trying to ask is, will you marry me?"

"Yes. Yes. Yes. Yes." I kneeled down to him and kissed all over his face. "Yes."

"Let's do this the right way then."

As we kissed in the middle of the floor, Lorena's drunk ass yelled, "Let's get this party started!"

Music instantly began to play on the surround sound and everyone spread apart.

"All food and drinks are paid for!" Ayshan yelled. "All food and drinks are paid for!"

"Man, you ain't have to do that," Poppa said to Saw as he rocked me side to side from behind.

"It's the least I could do. Congratulations, you two," he said as he made his way to where Khadijah sat.

"Nadia!" Marty yelled as he ran over to me.

"I'm your mama, boy," I said as I picked him up and held him tight. "What your gran say about me?" I asked in his ear.

"Stop that," Poppa said.

"She never even looked up."

"Who cares?"

"She hates me."

"Come on, let me introduce you to everyone." He grabbed my hand.

I dreaded going over where his family was because it was sooooo many of them, but I went anyway.

It took way too long for him to introduce me to all those people, whose names I would surely forget the minute I walked away from them.

After he introduced me to everyone, I broke away and mingled with Camille and Michael. "I can't believe you didn't tell me," I said as I grabbed his ear.

"I couldn't ruin your day."

"Give it to her," Camille said to him.

"Give me what?"

"As we cleaned out Mom's things, we found this." He handed me a picture of my mom when she was just a girl holding a baby. The baby was me.

"Oh my God." I held the picture close. No matter what transpired between me and her, she was still my mother and this picture was a part of history that I would always have now. "Thanks so much." I pulled them both in for a group hug.

"Jason wanted to make it but his child was christened today," Camille said. Wow. They chose to be here with me instead of seeing Jason's kid be christened. That meant a lot.

"You know why Wanda isn't here," Michael said.

"Yea, she sure knows how to hold a grudge, huh?" I asked.

"Yea. How dare you be born?" Camille joked.

"Right." I started to cry again and Camille held me tight.

"Don't cry. It's okay. It ain't perfect but it's family. Look around." She pulled back and held her hand out, pointing out to the gigantic crowd.

"It wasn't supposed to happen this way," I said. My mother was supposed to be here.

"Everything ain't perfect, Judy, but it's beautiful."

I laughed away tears as she wiped my face. "Yea, you right. It is beautiful."

Chapter 17
Judy
Take My Advice

A couple weeks had passed and everything seemed well, so I should've known something would go bad. But I didn't know what.

I was marrying the man of my dreams. Liyza was doing very well with her recovery. Nobody was questioning Tay's death. She had fucked so many people over that it was up for grabs who killed her. My son was walking and talking better. Nadia was happy and in Dubai with her big family. Lorena was getting her back blown out by Felipe. Camille, Michael, and I had a great relationship. Things couldn't get any better. But they damn sure could get worse and I was very cautious of that. I didn't have the best track record with keeping everything good.

I sat at a coffee shop enjoying the breeze and the view of the cattle across the way. Then I heard the chair across from me scratch against the tile. Someone sat down.

It was Wanda.

"Not today, Satan."

She pulled her shades down, revealing a semi-healed eye. "Satan? That's how you do me?"

"What do you want?"

"I want to apologize. Is that okay with you?"

"Now you want to apologize?" I laughed. "Please go to hell."

She grabbed my hand. "I'm serious."

"What do you want? Like for real?"

"I want to know your story. I never got to ask Mother about why she gave you up. Did she tell you?"

"Wanda, how the hell did you find me?"

"The cashier knows me. I come here often. Well, I used to. She told me you were here."

"And how does she know about us being related?"

"It's Austin. Word gets around fast."

"I guess."

"Please, Judy. I just want to try and fix this the best way we can. Mother's gone and so is my dad. You know what's it like to have nobody, I don't." I rolled my eyes at her. "I'm so sorry. That's so not how I meant for it to come out."

"You're a bitch without even trying. Hmph. Impressive."

She ordered a mocha and sat back. "I just didn't know our mother had it in her to have a child so young. She was only sixteen when she had you."

"Yes, she was. Her mother was also adopted so we don't have any extended family. I don't think I have to tell you that."

"I knew we didn't have other family on Mom's side but not because she was adopted."

"She told you they died in a car accident, huh?"

"How'd you know?"

"It's the most common lie people go with when they don't want to explain their family life. I used that same lie before I met our mom."

"She came looking for you?" She looked so sad when she asked. As if it would've deeply disappointed her if my mother had dared tried to find the child she lost.

"No, my fiancé took the initiative and found her. It was hard. Maybe her job made it so hard."

"Her job?"

"Yes."

"She worked as a social worker. I would think that made it easier." Oh my. So my mother really lived a double life. My poor siblings had no idea their mother was a cold-hearted bitch but also a loving mother.

"Right. I just thought it would be hard. You know?"

"I see. Who was your dad?"

Now that she was asking me, I hadn't thought about it. Mom told me months ago and I never thought twice about it.

My father was pastor at a church. He was older now but back then he was in his twenties. My mother went to him for help because she was being molested at her group home. So, he took her in and helped her...then molested her like the people she was running from. She had me and couldn't even look me in the eyes because they were identical to my father's. She once said if I was to ever meet him that I would know it's him because of his eyes. I hated him for what he did to my mom and what he turned her into, but he was the only family I had left.

"I don't know who my dad was," I lied. Last thing I needed was Wanda snooping around in my business. I didn't give a fuck what sister role she was trying so hard to play at the moment.

"I wish she would've told you. It would've given me more a clear view of who she was."

"You knew her. She raised you."

"Yea, but in the back of my mind, I feel like I didn't know her at all."

"Why?"

She shrugged her shoulders. "I mean, I'm married with a

kid and we found out about you. She had an entire life that we don't know about. Like, was she really even adopted?"

She had me thinking now. "That's what my fiancé said she told him."

"But what if she lied about that?"

"I don't think she would lie about that."

"Yea, but who knows? Right?"

"Right." I turned my gaze back out the window. I heard Wanda gathering her things to leave.

"Hey, I have a crazy question."

"What?"

"You didn't kill our mother, did you?"

"What...the fuck?"

"I know, I know. It was just that, the day she and dad went missing, I thought I heard her saying you were taking her to him."

"Na, wrong person."

"I know. I also thought I heard my dad say that our uncle was picking him up."

"How do you *think* to hear something?"

"I don't know. I'm crazy. Pay me no mind." She put her shades back on. "Oh, and your friend Lorena?"

"What about her?"

"I've been on her Facebook and her son is so handsome."

"Why are you on her page?"

"Wouldn't you want to know who beat your ass?" she said sarcastically. I saw what was going on. She felt played about being beat up so she was doing some major snooping.

"Not really."

"But her son, he's so handsome. He has a mole on the bottom of his lip like my father's side of the family has. All the boys have it. Even my brothers."

"That's nice."

"Yea. It's crazy. In an alternative world, maybe my father was having an affair with Lorena. She befriends you when she finds out your mother is his wife and you two kill her?"

I grabbed my purse and left some money on the table. "Bye, Wanda." If only she knew. She almost had it but she wasn't close. She had the wrong brother.

She followed close behind. "You have to admit, that's a nice story, huh?"

"Yep. Bye." I slid into my car and she grabbed the door handle, preventing me from shutting it.

"I will never know what happened to my my mother, *our mother*, but you need to watch your back."

"For who? Lorena?"

"Yes."

This was comical. "Because she befriended me to kill our mom, right?"

"Right. In another world maybe."

"Oh, okay. Cool story, except for one thing."

"What?"

"Lorena and I were friends far before me and Mom officially met."

She looked dumbfounded and backed away from my car like I wanted. "Something isn't right about their deaths, Judy, and you know it. Just help me get to the bottom of this. Please," she pleaded with her eyes.

I was looking for the most sweetest way to tell her to leave well enough alone. There wasn't anyone in my circle that I feared. I watched her uncle kill her dad in cold blood and then my mother. He didn't so much as blink. It was him who I feared her running this story by. Though she was way off, she was halfway right about Lorena's son. "Who else have you ran this theory by?"

"I have a few theories, but that's the only one makes sense."

"Who else?"

"Nobody."

"Wanda, if you believe our mother was murdered by some secret person, don't go around picking. If they killed them, supposedly, imagine what they'd do to you."

"I can't let it go. She was my mother. He was my father." Her face was flushed.

I didn't like her but I hated where I saw this going. "Wanda, please. Get some rest. You sound crazy."

"I'm not crazy. I promise."

I started the ignition to my car. "May God be with you, sister." I kissed her hand, truly feeling sad for her. She had no idea who she was dealing with. I wanted to tell her but I'd also learned to leave well enough alone. Gone were my days of complicating my life and the ones that I loved. Wanda would have to deal with this on her own.

Chapter 18
Judy
The Forever Thing

A few weeks later, I decided to try my luck with the man who raped my mom—my father.

Mom didn't lie. The minute I walked into the humongous church and took my seat, I knew exactly who my father was. Our eyes were identical and so was our skin color.

As he preached on the podium, his eyes caught mine and he froze. It's like he'd seen a ghost. "That's him, huh?" Lorena asked.

"Yep. Pastor Miller. Just like Mom said."

"Wow. So the bitch was truthful about some things."

"Yea, *some things.*"

"What you want to do?"

"We wait."

"Until after service?" she asked, disappointed.

I laughed. I didn't tell her we were staying the entire service. She never would've come if I told her that. "Yes. You'll be okay."

"No, I won't."

"Shhh. No talking," someone behind us said.

I just put my head down because I knew Lorena was about

to show her natural ass. "Who the fuck you talking to, old lady?"

"I can't hear."

"I was whispering to my friend. Is it my fault you were being nosey?"

The old woman didn't say anything else. I didn't want to turn around. If I turned around again, I would burst into laughter. That's not what I came for. "Stop, Lorena."

"Girl, fuck these people. They pastor a rapist." A few people gasped. Lorena also gasped but it was to mock the congregation.

"You so silly."

"Y'all upsetting me and my homegirl," Lorena said to someone on side of us who was also being nosey.

"I ain't mad, bitch. I'm laughing," I said.

"Well, y'all upsetting me," she corrected herself.

"I will buy you drinks next weekend if you relax. Please."

She crossed her legs and popped her collar. "Well, since you put it that way." She cleared her throat.

We sat quietly the rest of the show.

"Let the church say Amen," Pastor Miller said, finishing up his sermon."

"Amen, Pastor Daddy," Lorena said.

"She needs to leave," I heard someone say under their breath.

"Make me leave," Lorena said.

"Please bow your heads," Pastor Miller said.

I grabbed Lorena's hand tightly, trying so hard not to laugh while it was quiet. She and I together were like two children on a playground.

After everyone was dismissed and the crowd thinned, we made our way to the back where they said his office was. Luckily, we caught him just in time. It seemed as if he was expecting us to walk through that door.

He didn't immediately speak when we came in and sat down. He lifted his fat self from the chair and locked the door to his office first. "I always knew this day would come," he said, staring into my eyes.

"I'm Judy."

"She never told me about you, but I heard the rumors." He pulled his hands together in a praying way. "And here you come walking through my office door. You have her features but my eyes. How is she? Is she okay?"

"You haven't watched the news, huh?"

"Too much killing. Stopped decades ago."

"She's dead's, she died months ago."

"Oh no. I hadn't seen her since the day she left my home."

"Maybe because you raped her."

I expected him to deny it and get upset, but he didn't. "I'm not perfect. I gave her a choice."

"To sleep with you or to be homeless?" He didn't answer. "Some choice."

"Your mother came to this church over two decades ago when my father was the pastor. She asked for help with an abortion and my father turned her away because he didn't believe in abortions."

"Wait, what?"

"Yes. There was a baby before you but she didn't keep it. Once I found out who the father was, I helped her immediately."

"Who was the father?"

"Your grandfather."

"Her father?" I clarified.

"Yes. He's still doing time for what he did to them."

"Them?"

Pastor Miller looked taken aback. "You have no idea where you come from, do you?"

"I don't. Not completely."

"Her father killed her mother, your grandmother, and held Cat captive for days."

"I feel like I have to puke," Lorena said.

My poor mother. She went through so much just to meet an end so violent. Look what life did to her. It did the same thing to her that it did to Maddy. "So you helped her get an abortion just to rape her?"

He put his head down. "Like I said, I'm not proud of my actions, but I didn't abuse your mother. I allowed her to live with me when her father was arrested. Your mother had abandonment issues so she cuddled up under people at night to make sure they wouldn't leave in the morning. See, I didn't know this back then. Back then, I thought she wanted a sex."

"She was a girl. You were a man."

"I know. It wasn't until later when I realized how wrongly I had misread that situation. She left the next day and I never saw her again, but I heard rumors of a child gave up. I searched and searched but never could find you. I heard she named you Athedra but when I searched for that child, I never found it. So my only guess was she either took you with her when she went away or she never had you and it was all rumors."

"Wow. Do you know where she went after that?"

"No idea. I just heard she was married to the mayor's brother, but she never showed herself to me ever again."

"Do I have any siblings? This ain't ideal, but you're the only family I have left."

"Of course, you have siblings, but I also know who your grandparents other children were."

My face beamed with joy. "I have aunts? Uncles? Cousins?"

"Yes. You have quite a few of them. You've been a rumor for many years and to see you standing here in the flesh is like a dream." He stood. "Can I give you a hug?"

"Yes." I wiped my tears and ran around to him. "It still doesn't take away what you did with a minor."

"I know, it's no excuse. None whatsoever. Even though a four-year age gap was accepted back then, I had no right. I took complete advantage. I just wish instead of leaving she could've talked to me about it. I was and still am a very reasonable man. It would've never happened again. I truly loved and cared about your mother. She'd gone through so much with men, I think she feared I may have reacted how her dad did, and I will forever be sorry to her and you."

"She was amazing."

"Bullshit," Lorena said under her breath.

"Never mind her."

"It took the power of the Holy Ghost for me not to stop my sermon and fall out laughing at your friend."

"She's something else." I wiped the rest of my tears. I couldn't believe this was actually happening. My life was so tragic and beautiful. Maybe the tragic parts were what made it beautiful.

"Would you like to meet your sister? She's a couple years older."

"Where is she?"

"She was the one sitting behind you two that told your friend to be quiet."

"The old lady?" I asked.

"She's not old. She just has an old soul and wears far too much makeup."

"I would love to meet her."

"I'm telling you now, she's a tough cookie." He grabbed his phone and keys.

"I can handle it."

He led us down the hall and introduce me to everyone at the church.

Before leaving, we exchanged numbers and I left. I even invited him to my wedding.

Yet and still, Lorena was not impressed. "I don't like your sister," she said.

"Yea, I don't think we will get along."

"Big hat wearing ass. She need to lose some weight."

"She smelled like onions, huh? I thought it was just me who smelled it."

"No ma'am. I smelled that shit. She so busy worrying about me, when she needed to be bathing."

"You must be on your period?" I asked.

"How you know?"

"You're cranky today."

"Just started too."

"You need some dick."

"Hours' worth. I need some baby daddy dick but ever since I started dating, he won't have sex with me."

"Really? What a jerk."

"Right. It's like he thinks I'm not responsible. He's the sex addict, not me."

"I wonder who he's sticking it too now."

"Hopefully just his wife."

"I doubt it," I said. "Maybe some black girl."

"Maybe."

I dropped her off and then made my way back home to tell Poppa about my day. He was sitting on the couch, waiting. He knew I had an earful.

"Where's Marty?"

"Napping. I let him play until he tired himself out."

"It's so early."

"So what?"

"Never mind. So he's indeed my father." I plopped next to him.

"He really raped your mom?"

"I would say it was a misunderstanding." I then broke it down to him.

"I mean, I still think it was wrong because she was a teenager but back then, women were getting married at fifteen and sixteen."

"That's what he said."

"Any family?"

"Turns out my mom told the truth about my dad but lied about her parents."

"What you mean?"

"She knew who they where."

"Word?"

"Yea. And you were right, her story was tragic. It was very tragic."

"What happened?"

I then explained to him what my grandfather did and how he was still in prison right now for what he did.

"Damn. That's fucked up."

"Very." I cuddled under him. "Lorena almost slapped my sister."

"Lorena has a problem keeping her hands to herself. Did you call Camille back?"

"Na, I'll call later."

"So do you like him? Your dad?"

"Yea. He made me feel very welcome. He even laughed off Lorena and her attitude. He's a very gentle man. I just wish my mom was here to get the closure she needed. You know? I wish she could've lived to know that he wasn't a monster."

"I think she knew that."

"Why you say that?"

"She wouldn't have told you the truth about him if he was a monster. Her dad was a monster and she lied about him, but she told the truth about the pastor."

I kissed his forehead. "When you put it like that, I guess you're right."

"I'm happy for you, pretty girl."

"Thank you, baby."

"You sure you want the wedding to be this fall?"

"Yes. Why?"

"I'm bringing my entire family here. Needed to be sure."

"Here? Like in our home? Hell to the na. We ain't doing that shit again."

He chuckled. "Who you telling? It's too many of them. I was going to rent out the villa for them. I don't even think the villa will be big enough."

"Don't forget it has a guest house."

"Why do I keep forgetting that?"

"I don't know. It wasn't that long ago that we were there."

"It's about to be a year since we left. It's been a minute."

"Man, it has been almost a year. Look how much happened."

"Right," he said.

"Nadia had a whole baby and now her family lives in Dubai. No lie, I ain't see that shit coming."

"Your dad being a preacher? I ain't see that coming."

"The mayor and Saw being friends? I didn't see that coming," I said.

"Your mother being killed by the mayor? Yea, definitely didn't see that coming."

"The mayor killing his brother? I didn't see that coming."

"Your sister Wanda getting her ass beat by Lorena? I ain't see that coming."

"Lorena being a loyal friend to me? I ain't see that coming."

"Liyza sucking dick? Yeaaa, I definitely ain't see that coming."

"Me neither. Shit, I don't think anyone could've seen that coming and I've been knowing her all my life. She's talking about having babies, bruh."

"Ew," he said.

"Hey, not too much on her. Not too much."

"You know it's true. Liyza doesn't look like the submissive type." He grabbed my feet and rubbed them until I relaxed more.

"She said she lets him take the lead during sex."

"Please stop."

"She said she likes being bent over," I continued. "She's still a woman, Poppa."

"That's a grown ass man."

"She's a broken woman and is finding her way." I smiled.

"Man, that's the damn homie."

"You so silly. What we eating today? I don't feel like cooking."

"I ordered pizza. It should be here soon."

"How you know I wasn't going to feel like cooking?"

"Because I know my wife."

"Damn."

"What?"

"You've been referring to me as your wife?"

"Yea, why?"

"My bad, big dog."

"What?"

"I been telling people you my fiancé."

"So ain't your husband?"

"We ain't married yet."

"We signed the papers. By law, you're my wife."

"You my baby daddy."

"Damn. When you gotta act like this?" he asked, laughing.

"Like what? Until we walk down the aisle, you my baby daddy."

"Man, fuck them folks. You my wife. Stop calling me your damn baby daddy."

There was a knock at the door. I hurried to grab the pizza because I was that hungry. When the pizza lady handed the box over, I remembered I didn't have my wallet on me. "Hold on. Let me get some money from my baby daddy."

"Stop calling me your damn baby daddy!"

The lady laughed as I walked away. "Where your wallet?" I asked, putting the pizza down.

"On the counter."

It was right in my face. I paid for the pizza and took my bra off, ready to dive in. He took the cheesy slice I had from me and moved the box away. "Stoooooop! I'm hungry."

"Call me your husband."

"Your husband. Now give me the pizza."

He ate the pizza in my face and smacked on it. "Um, this so good. I'd sure hate to eat this whole thing in your face."

"Okay, you're my husband."

"Now kiss me."

I kissed him and attempted to jack the pizza but he was too fast. "Poppa!"

"What I say?"

"Husband."

"Na, you don't mean that."

"Poppa, come on, I'm about to cry. I haven't eaten since last night. Please."

"Na. You need to be to taught a lesson."

My eyes watered and he burst into laughter. "You triggered?"

"Give me the food, Poppa, damn."

"I'm annoying you?"

"Yes!"

"Good. I'm about to annoy you for the rest of your life."

"I don't care, just give me the pizza."

"Here, big crybaby." He placed the box in my lap and watched as I tore into the box. I damn near tore a slice of the box and ate it.

As I ate the food, Marty came into the living room and crawled into my lap, making me move the pizza. He then laid down and went to sleep. Out of all places, he wanted to move my pizza and lay in my lap.

Though I was annoyed, this was the perfect Sunday that I didn't even know I needed.

"Can you grab me a juice, husband? I don't want to wake him."

"Oh, I'm husband now?"

"Yes."

He shook his head and walked to the kitchen. "Women. Man I tell ya."

"Can't live without us."

"I can't live without you. I can live without them other hoes. They annoying."

"You don't even try to be funny and that's what makes you funny."

"I was serious as hell. Damn, that's fucked up," he said.

"What?"

"It's a nigga out here right now watching Liyza get naked."

I popped his arm. "Boy, leave my damn friend alone."

"I'm just playing." He leaned over and poked his lips out for a kiss.

"Muah." I made the sound effects as I kissed him.

"I love you, pretty girl."

"I love you too."

He pulled me close and we watched TV together. I could do this forever thing. It was pretty cool.

The end

Follow Kia Jones

Follow Kia Jones on social media to keep up with the latest: IG: LoraineLavelle

Also by Kia Jones

Made in the USA
Columbia, SC
04 October 2023

23916764R00079